PRAISE

"Ravishing . . . as if Saavedra were a modern-day Borges. Translated brilliantly from the Portuguese by Daniel Hahn, *Blue Flowers* plays out in a musical dance between A.'s letters and the slow immolation of Marcos's world as he grows addicted to them. It's a mystery, yes. It might be a ghost story. It is sexy, and often unsettling. By the end, you could be forgiven for chewing your fingernails, wondering whether it's all a figment of Marcos's imagination. Or not."   —Luis Alberto Urrea,
O, the Oprah Magazine

"A story of obsession and the underside of desire."
—*The New York Times*

"Saavedra, a lauded Brazilian writer, twists this search deftly. As A.'s correspondence unfolds, it explores language's insufficiencies, and its power."   —*The New Yorker*

"Saavedra's writing, particularly in the raw and vulnerable epistles, feels relentless and evocative in Hahn's translation and creates intensity inside this tale shaped by characters strongly preoccupied with words and meaning. Thematically layered and psychologically demanding, this is a book for readers willing to explore uneasy relationship dynamics."
—*Booklist*

"Captivating . . . In chapters alternating between letters and Marcos's reactions, Saavedra steadily unveils the darkness permeating the lives of her protagonists, and in doing so creates a literary psychological thriller that questions what is real and what is imagined. This tale of desire and yearning is impossible to put down."   —*Publishers Weekly*

"*Blue Flowers* is an elegant and unnerving meditation on the aftermath of love and the lasting power of desire. It's a bracing, fast read, one with a long afterglow and a dangerous lesson: that it may be that distance and removal are the only ways to learn about presence and proximity."   —Catherine Lacey, author of *The Answers* and *Nobody Is Ever Missing*

"An enchanting and disturbing epistolary monologue charged with danger, mystery, desire, and longing, as seen through the eyes of a woman with nothing left to lose. This novel reminded me of Marais and Carrère in all the best ways—but better, and deeper, for its honesty and pure feeling. I can't stop thinking about it."   —Lisa Locascio, author of *Open Me*

"Saavedra confirms her talent by using devices from the epistolary genre and transforming the reader into an accomplice in a plot full of tricks."   —*O Estado de S. Paulo* (Brazil)

"An astounding book."   —*Gazeta do Povo* (Brazil)

BLUE
FLOWERS

CAROLA SAAVEDRA

Translated by Daniel Hahn

Riverhead Books   New York

RIVERHEAD BOOKS
An imprint of Penguin Random House LLC
penguinrandomhouse.com

First published as *Flores azuis* by Companhia das Letras, Brazil, 2008
First American edition published by Riverhead Books, 2020
Copyright © 2008 by Carola Saavedra
Translation copyright © 2020 by Daniel Hahn

The Library of Congress has catalogued
the Riverhead hardcover edition as follows:

Names: Saavedra, Carola, 1973– author. | Hahn, Daniel, translator.
Title: Blue flowers / Carola Saavedra ; translated by Daniel Hahn.
Other titles: Flores azuis. English.
Description: New York : Riverhead Books, 2020. |
Identifiers: LCCN 2019013028 (print) | LCCN 2019016797 (ebook) |
ISBN 9781594631757 (hardcover) | ISBN 9781101624029 (ebook)
Classification: LCC PQ9698.429.A2 (ebook) |
LCC PQ9698.429.A2 F5313 2020 (print) | DDC 869.3/5—dc23
LC record available at https://lccn.loc.gov/2019013028

First Riverhead hardcover edition: January 2020
First Riverhead trade paperback edition: January 2021
Riverhead trade paperback ISBN: 9780593086865

Printed in the United States of America
1   3   5   7   9   10   8   6   4   2

Book design by Daniel Lagin

BLUE FLOWERS

My darling,

They say separation is never one single moment; it's never abrupt. They say a separation starts inside out. It's precisely at the moment of greatest sweetness—at that first meeting, at that first look—that a separation begins to exist. I prefer to believe a separation never ends, and that the last day, the last night, is a moment that is repeated again and again with every return, every time I feel your absence, every time I speak your name. I believe that when I call out to you, I should be able to make you turn and look, and without realizing it, create a bridge between us.

But how do I call out to someone who has gone? Someone who is far away, who is not here? Distance should immediately impose a more solemn tone, or a less intimate one; there's a distance there, after all. But how should I behave distantly toward someone who just a moment ago was so close beside me, so recently lying beside me in my bed? Every day, every night, we had something as intimate as sharing a bed. When the day breaks, the sheets are thrown open, all crumpled up, stained and infused with the shared night. How does a person move out of our bed and into a kind of stiff formality?

I imagine at this moment you're there in your apartment, on your sofa, in your favorite armchair or the regular chair left carelessly by the kitchen table. You're just sitting there with a glass of water, a cup of coffee. This letter is in your hands and you ask yourself, perhaps with a bit of irritation, why this isn't over after all. Why didn't you leave, why go on like this, why go on with the leaving, indefinitely, you could be asking yourself. My answer to you is that I don't know, unless maybe there's some need to recover something unrecoverable; what other reason could there be? This is my attempt at preventing you from getting up, going over to shut the window or even answering the phone. The phone might ring, someone might wave from the balcony opposite, the insistent noise of the telephone, but still you sit there, apart, silent, this letter in your hands—your hands that I fear and also love, and that I wish were now gentle—feeling the smoothness or the roughness of these pages and the ripple of the imperceptible fibers being born and being undone again, in constant motion. But perhaps some things really are unrecoverable.

Perhaps everything is unrecoverable, everything, not only the past, which is lost to memory, but the present, the now which seems so alive, so precise. And—even if I should want it, even if I really try—perhaps even me, even you. Sad, isn't it? I try to imagine the expression on your face, your face, your mouth, your gaze at this moment, now, now, this moment that is no more than a space, an intense emptiness separating us, the distance between my hands and yours, between my fingers wandering over this keyboard, and yours caressing the texture of the paper. You, sitting in an armchair or on a chair or on the sofa, in the apartment I know so well, holding the words I choose, the individual letters, the linked phrases trampled down by time, by this constant aging. How to traverse this distance that separates us? This interval between what I say and what you read, this moment that never arrives, that never is?

I think about your face when I used to ask you a question, any old bit of nonsense. Your face would be tense, apprehensive, at the pointlessness of my questions. You never realized that I was asking without expecting any answer, just out of a simple need to confirm that you were there with me, my hand seeking yours, seeking any affection, any tenderness for me on your part. Like those children who run through the house looking for their mother who's disappeared with no warning, their mother who's gone to the kitchen, to the bedroom or out onto the porch to see what the weather's like or to wave to someone, their mother who, all of a sudden, never suspecting, transforms into someone not there, someone who's disappeared. All that remains is the child's world and the mother's absence. And somebody searching in the dark for any sign of tenderness, trying constantly to ascertain something, like the child who knows nothing more than what they are able to perceive. That's it, that's what I'm like now, nothing exists except what I am able to perceive. And even if you concealed your absence, even if you tried to disguise it, it was as if you weren't there, as if you were always in another room, in the kitchen, on the porch, waving to someone who's walking past and I have no idea who they are.

So, my insistence, and this letter. And you, even if only for a few moments, even if only a shadow, a mere movement. I turn in alarm, looking around me, imagining your presence here, unexpected, inexplicable. Because there is something I want to tell you, something that was abandoned half-finished, a house left empty or an incomplete phrase or some kind of loaded silence, as if silences could mean something, or perhaps because silences mean whatever we want them to. Because there was something left half-finished. Something that will come later. Because there are things that take their time to start existing. And that need repeating, again and again. Separation.

I haven't left the house for days. I've told you that already, I have, haven't I? If I were that sort of woman, I could even be dramatic, tell you I haven't left the house for days, haven't eaten for days, haven't washed, haven't combed my hair, you remember that, my hair, which you used to like me to wear loose, remember? Which you used to praise, you used to say it looked like a dark curtain, dark as a bird, dark as the night; did you ever say such a thing, I wonder? No, you never would have said anything like that. But no, I'm not going to tell you I'm suffering, what would be the point? Better to tell you about other things. I haven't left the house for days, haven't washed, haven't combed my hair. Days. I wonder if I'm forgetting something important?

I've always suspected that we tend to forget the most important moment, perhaps because it's a target in a constant state of transformation; the most important moment is always something else, something that eludes us. Like that space I was telling you about, between what I write and what you read. Something that creates a disturbance, without ever taking shape. What great dangers this can bring, as the transformation into words takes shape into a kind of witness, or a sign. And if there is no danger, I could very easily tell you about yesterday, or perhaps tell you a secret, or a very intimate desire, or something that might reveal me. I could tell you, for example, about yesterday.

Yesterday I thought of you: my mouth on your mouth and your hands in my hair and your body next to mine. Remember? Your body next to mine and all the things that could do to me. The constant falling. The brushing against your skin, the smoothnesses and roughnesses of your skin. My nervous breathing, just like now, at this moment when I write to you and remember—remember? Our imaginary geography: your body next to mine. The strength of your demanding voice, your voice a caress, next to me, in my ear, your voice, remember? Your name in the farthest corners, in the subtlest areas of my body, remember? My body falling, like now, because it was yours, your hand that ran over me, your fingers startling me, running over the skin inside my thighs and wrapping around my belly and my waist, and your voice kissing the back of my neck, and your voice behind me, and me losing myself and finding myself again, in you, like now, as if everything about me were water. Your name next to mine, my name, your wanting. I dissolve away and say yes, that I am yours, your woman, your whatever you want.

But maybe you don't remember, and all that's left is an imperfect gesture, a doubt. Perhaps you don't want all this revelation, all this intimacy. This excess of words. Perhaps. So I will move away and start again: yesterday.

Yesterday I went to the DVD rental place on the corner near home. And finally, as it takes shape, do you remember that last day? First thing in the morning, when we went to that rental place together, your hand refused mine. Remember what you said to me as we went in? Perhaps you don't remember, you there, on the other side of the story now, in your armchair with your cup of coffee, perhaps you don't remember, but no matter.

And since I'm the one writing, I am the one who gets to choose and tell you how it was, and this is how it was: It was summer, it was a hot day, we were walking side by side, we were talking about the previous night's dinner, something had happened and it was bothering you, wasn't it? Our voices were muffled by the noise of the cars, the people with their newspapers and bread and milk they'd just bought. Something was bothering you. It was Saturday, and we went into the rental place; the attendant behind the counter barely noticed our arrival. As we came in, we were relieved at the sudden silence and the coolness of the air-conditioning. You moved away and I stayed where I was, running my eyes over the shelves, looking for a movie I'd been wanting to show you for a while, a very special movie, I mentioned mysteriously, though you were barely paying attention. You kept walking, saying something about the night before, about the dinner, something that was bothering you. I'd like you to see this movie, I said again, I held the case out to you, commenting, without thinking too much of it, that the main character was a lot like you: Even the actor looks like you, don't you think? You stopped for a moment, serious all of a sudden, said nothing, the movie case in your hands. You were silent. Then you asked, Like me in what way? I didn't think too much of it, my eyes still on the shelves, but you had a troubled expression, something I didn't understand. Like me in what way?

The movie was in your hands. The look on your face was not merely distant, but a look that closed and enclosed within it a flash of light, the discovery of a secret. I don't know, I replied, and I remember you were still trying to contain that rage, that aggression—where could it have come from? Like me in what way? you insisted. And I barely thought of it but just in order to say something, I said, The way people sometimes look like someone you saw once, someplace, and you keep thinking yes, I know them from somewhere, without ever finding out from where. A déjà vu, I concluded. You looked closely at the cover of the movie, the photo of the actor, a dark man with a handsome though coarse-looking face, in sharp contrast with a blond woman in the image, very fragile, lying on a bed. You insisted, What are you implying? your tone aggressive. And I hadn't meant to imply anything, because it didn't mean anything, I had just said it in order to say something, so I asked, Why does everything have to mean something? You said you knew the movie very well, and no, you were nothing alike, you and the character, still less the actor, his face handsome though coarse. I smiled, though not amused, and began to turn my face away, an imperceptible flight. Like so many other times, now that I think about it, ever since the beginning of us, our beginning, you had that hatred, that rage, but why?

You were pissed off, hostile, and dragged me by the arm out of the rental place. I could feel my breathing unsettled, wild. You dragged me outside. I wanted to insist on going back, to say it didn't mean anything, that I'd said it just to say something. And that I was also angry, that I could do whatever I saw fit, watch any movie I wanted to, you hear me? But you squeezed my arm unexpectedly hard, and I felt that my arm was just an extension, an appendix. It felt as though you hated me, as though suddenly you hated me and wanted to hurt me. Yes, that's what I think, as though you wanted to hurt me very much, very deeply. And like that, your fingers buried in my arm, you said something I didn't understand, you spoke looking off toward nothingness, and all I remember was the end of the phrase: Not now, you hear me? You hear me? I felt my body surrender and shake all over, submissive, delicate, bending under the weight of your hand, my whole body, the pressure of your fingers, and you said again, your lips almost shut: Not now, you hear me?

Later, on the street, the two of us walked quickly, you were dragging me as though you wanted to pull me over.

I went with you, carried by an incomprehensible force, this incomprehensible force that was your will, that was you. I was feeling as though at any moment I might give up and start screaming, right there in the middle of the street, start crying inconsolably for what, I didn't quite know, but from which, I knew, there was no way to recover.

But no, that's not what happened in the end; it's funny, it never is. I didn't cry, and I didn't scream, and I didn't say anything. You went on, your fingers digging into my arm, with quick and determined steps, and I went on, more and more submissive beside you, with quick and determined steps. That was our last day. Remember?

I remember, and I'm remembering again now. In spite of the waiting, in spite of time, in spite of the gap separating us. There is always a word uniting us. Now, my fingers on the keys. Now, you reading this on the sofa, in the armchair. These words uniting us.

A.

I

When he'd finished reading the letter, he put it back into the envelope and left it on the table, standing a moment in silence, feeling strange, unsettled. He looked at the little girl who was lying on the living room rug, drawing a picture, the rain outside never-ending. He decided to forget about the letter, to forget the whole business.

Instead, he wondered how to distract a child on a rainy day, wondered about maybe phoning for a pizza, wondered whether it was perhaps still too early for lunch. He considered calling his ex-wife to suggest a family lunch. No, he wouldn't do that. She'd get the wrong idea, and he was very happy with the way things were. He considered calling Fabiane, who would eagerly welcome a call from him. No, the presence of the child would make any meeting seem too much like an invitation, something with family and potential.

He went back to thinking about the letter, still a little confused; the truth was that he had just read a letter meant for someone else, had intimate access to someone else. He felt both unsettled and attracted to this correspondence that did not belong to him. It would never have crossed his mind to open a letter that wasn't for him, and now there was this indiscretion, this curiosity, which intrigued him; perhaps it was the light blue envelope, the writing in black ink, with a fountain pen. He recognized this at once, remembering one he'd had when he was a child, a gift from his grandfather; he found it strange that anyone should still write with a fountain pen, that anyone should still be writing letters at all.

In the place of a sender's name, just that letter *A.* No address, nothing. Before opening it, he had already guessed that A. was a woman, perhaps because of the attractive, rounded hand, perhaps because of the letter itself. At the time he justified opening the envelope with an assurance that he had no way of returning it—who would he return it to? And he opened it to see whether he might discover some clue, some name, some address, he thought, as though excusing himself. He kept thinking about the letter for a few moments longer, until the girl called out to him:

"Dad?"

"What, Manuela?"

"Dad, look!"

The girl brought over a piece of paper.

"Dad, look what I drew."

He took the drawing, looked it over carefully, a circular shape and a few undefined scribbles crisscrossing it. He held on to the piece of paper somewhat unsure, and perhaps his expression was a little doubtful; the girl pointed, insisting.

"Dad, look."

"How lovely, sweetie. Is it me?"

"No, it's Felipe."

"Oh, Felipe—really good. Really, yes, it's beautiful."

He felt just a touch of jealousy that, sure, of course, Felipe, even the cat was more important than her own father. Right away he felt ridiculous, comparing himself to the cat. The girl came closer and held out her hand.

"Give it to me."

"What do you want, the picture?"

"Yeah."

He handed the sheet back to her. He was still thinking about Felipe, the cat she had been given right after the separation, a goggle-eyed black cat. His ex-wife, hoping to compensate for any trauma and maybe even to distract the girl, had gotten her the animal, a cat with a person's name. The girl had chosen the name herself, and where she'd gotten "Felipe" from he would never know; it was just one of those kid things, his ex-wife explained with an ironic smile. Fine. Felipe. No one had notified him, no one had asked his opinion. His ex-wife made him feel like a stranger.

He looked at his daughter, a redhead with very pale, curly hair, three years old. He could hardly believe it when he thought about it, that he was the father of a three-year-old girl, how could such a thing have happened. Being a father was like waking up one day on a different planet, with no warning, no time to prepare, nothing. Waking up one day completely normally and all of a sudden being a father, with all the demands of being a father. In truth, he was never going to get used to it. And now here she was, here by his side on weekends. He had tried to explain that he didn't have the time, too much work he said, but his ex-wife complained, Don't forget she's your daughter, too. Sure, he wasn't going to forget. And so there she was, and soon the girl would get bored of drawing, and that rain outside was going to be a problem; on sunny days at least there was the beach. He had to think of getting something to eat, a pizza.

"Manuela, what do you think about us going out for a pizza?"

The girl ignored him, focused on her sheet of paper. He remained silent, he never knew what to say to his daughter, and he thought she looked at him with suspicion. She cried each time her mother left. He felt awful; the girl didn't like him. His ex-wife explained that it was because he didn't like the cat. And it was true, he really didn't like the cat—he'd never had pets, a cat, dog, hamster, parrot, those animals that are good for nothing but racking up bills and creating messes. He wouldn't have known what to do with a cat, but his ex-wife managed to make him feel guilty for not wanting his daughter's beloved cat to get his apartment all dirty.

It's very complicated being a father. Who's to say that children are necessarily going to like their parents? he wondered sadly. Children ought to come with an instruction manual. Pregnant women, too. During the pregnancy he'd gone with his ex-wife to a parenting course, all the men so proud, stroking their partners' bellies. Those huge bellies, all out of proportion. There he was, feeling quite wrong about it from beginning to end. He couldn't find it beautiful, that belly, his wife with her legs swollen, her round face; she seemed strange to him, as though he didn't know her, or as though she were hiding something from him the whole time. His wife would complain that he was distant, that he wasn't paying her any attention, that he wasn't interested in the pregnancy, in the baby, that he didn't even touch her. But no one had asked his opinion, after all. One day she had just shown up pregnant, happy—she'd prepared a special dinner just to tell him, pregnant and happy with a radiant smile. And then weeping because his smile hadn't been as radiant as hers. Women were like that, he thought, when they wanted something they didn't care, they didn't ask, they just went off and did it, and then they felt deeply disappointed when other people didn't share their excitement. The girl was still drawing.

"Aren't you hungry, Manuela? Let's go get a pizza, that ham pizza you really like, don't you want one of those?"

"No."

The girl shook her head as though needing to accentuate her no with a gesture. Lying there on the rug, her colored pencils scattered all over the room, with a drawing pad he'd given her as a present, all her attention was focused on another portrait of Felipe.

He picked up the letter again. It had arrived that same day, that morning. He had just woken up, and taking advantage of the fact that the girl was still sleeping, he'd put on a T-shirt, a pair of shorts and flip-flops, picked up an umbrella and gone down to buy something for breakfast. He hadn't even looked in the mailbox, and only on the way back had he remembered that thing he'd ordered online. Not yet. But there was the letter.

It was a light blue envelope, with the name of someone who wasn't him written in a careful, rounded hand, and underneath it was his address, written exactly right, and at the top was a stamp commemorating something he couldn't make out, franked by the mail, dated the previous day. In the place where the sender's name would normally go was merely the initial *A.*, no address, no other clue. He couldn't remember the last time he had received a letter, he thought, perhaps when he was a kid, a teenager, maybe he'd never received a personal letter, and he found this idea kind of funny, imagining that this really might be his first. And if it really was his first, it wasn't addressed to him, he thought, as he stored it away in the plastic supermarket bag.

When he had come into the apartment that morning, he shut the door and put everything down on top of the table. The girl must still be asleep. He took the envelope, examined it again, a heavy envelope; clearly a long letter, he thought. He left it on the side table, next to the phone and the previous days' correspondence. He went over to the kitchen, put the water to boil, set the table for when the girl woke up, arranged what he had bought: bread, cheese, jam. He rarely ate anything himself before midday, but his ex-wife never tired of giving him all manner of instructions for the girl: that she should eat properly, that she shouldn't have too much junk, always the same. When the coffee was ready, he poured himself a cup and went into the living room. He took up the letter and sat at the table.

Of course he shouldn't open a letter that wasn't for him. But it could be important, he thought. Yes, it was definitely something important. It wasn't some anonymous letter, the addressee might have been well aware of who A. was. Who would go to all the trouble of writing a letter in this day and age? Most likely a woman. And then there was that rounded handwriting. And yet, how could he even be sure it really was a letter? It could be anything, a document, a magazine clipping. Yet, for some reason, he was sure it was a letter, he knew it all along. Just as those thoughts began to appear, he was simultaneously assailed by a certain feeling of unease, the recollection of nosy old ladies leaning out of their windows, asking where have you been, where are you going. Best to forget the whole business. He would hand the letter over to the doorman, he'd know what to do with it, most likely the addressee was the former tenant of the apartment, he hadn't been here long, after all. No doubt the doorman knew who the person was, how to track him down. He put the letter back onto the table and decided to read the newspaper.

He was already on his second cup of coffee when the girl woke up. She came into the living room, tottering slightly.

"Hey, Manuela, good morning."

The girl didn't reply, she headed for the TV and sat down on the sofa, not yet fully awake. On the screen were fantastical beings, hybrids, chimeras, nothing he could recognize. If cartoons had only been the same as the ones parents watched as children, communicating with kids would be a whole lot easier. Conversation would come right away, naturally, a mix of eagerness and nostalgia, without that anxiety, that effort to do something the child would find interesting. Without the need for a cat getting the apartment all dirty. There had to be some kind of training course, How to Talk to a Child. Nobody ever thought of things like that.

"Come over here, Manuela, let's get some breakfast."

The girl didn't reply, her eyes glued to the TV.

"Come on, you can go back to watching your cartoon later."

She was ignoring him, he thought a little impatiently, were all children like this? What was he supposed to do, force her to sit at the table with him, argue, turn authoritarian, an attitude he himself had so often criticized in his own parents? And if she were to cry, that would be even worse, for sure. She was an atypical child, she almost never cried, she was hardly any trouble at all, but she had that look in her eyes, a challenging look that made him feel uncomfortable, inadequate. How was it possible that a three-year-old girl should manage to make him feel that way, his own daughter? It was as though she demanded something of him, something he had no idea about and had no way of giving to her. He felt guilty. Maybe that's what it is, he thought, guilt. He chose instead to go to the kitchen himself; he prepared her a glass of chocolate milk. He came back, this time trying a more determined tone of voice.

"Here, Manuela, drink this."

The girl did as she was told, she took the glass and started drinking. He considered making her say thank you but decided against it. He wasn't the only one at fault, after all, there was also her mother, his ex-wife, who wasn't bringing her up right. He'd say this to her as soon as he got the chance. He sensed that any moment now the girl was going to spill the cup of milk on the sofa. She was distracted from the whole world. He went back to reading the paper. From time to time, he thought about the letter again. He spent the whole morning like this. The girl watched TV, the glass still half full on the coffee table, while he read the paper, wondering whether or not to open the letter.

He ended up opening it. He took the envelope and sat

down at the dining table. The girl had given up on TV and decided to do some drawing, she'd scattered the colored pencils all over the rug. He opened the envelope carefully. White paper, five sheets printed from a computer, he looked unhurriedly for the signature, also typed, just the initial. He found it odd that the letter hadn't been handwritten, after all what was the point of going to the trouble of going to the post office to send a letter if it wasn't for that intimacy, real handwriting, those little revelations, like on the envelope, he thought, feeling strangely cheated, it was denying him a confidence, that rounded handwriting. The same hand that had written his address and that name that wasn't his. The black ink on the blue envelope, ink from a fountain pen, he knew, not from a ballpoint, maybe that was it, that detail, he'd recognized it at once, the fountain pen, fingers that always ended up getting stained, maybe that was what made him so curious. It ought to have been handwritten, he thought, a little disappointed. He began to read; the letter was addressed to someone she called "my darling." It was a love letter.

JANUARY 20

My darling,

I've spent the day thinking about the letter I wrote yesterday, about your reaction. Did you read it, I wonder.
Nervously opening the envelope while you were still in
the elevator, or maybe you threw it away, before you'd
even arrived back home, the envelope intact, or maybe
you tore it up, the pieces in the trash can out in the hallway, along with all the other pieces of paper, advertise-
ments, scribblings, newspapers, everything that nobody
wanted, or maybe you just left the envelope still closed
on the table, the day going by and the envelope on the
table, silent. I've spent the day thinking. And if you really
did read it, if you arrived home, opened the envelope
and read it, what happened? Did you hear me, I wonder?
Did you understand even the most unexpected parts
of my narrative, did you understand, I wonder? Did it

bring us closer? Did those memories, something of ours, return to existence, or is it maybe only me, all me, the desire, the writing, the reading. Perhaps I call out to you, and you go on, never looking back. And I keep on thinking whether there was something that could have caught you, there, where you are, wherever you are now.

It is also possible you didn't like it, that maybe you hate me even more now. That I made you recall our last day, our trip to the rental place, that I forced you to re-member and maybe you don't want to. Maybe you'd just rather keep looking ahead into the future, to whatever's coming. Believing that separation is an ending, not an eternal moment, as I would like to believe.

You are someone different, someone who walks down the street without ever looking back. Maybe you hate me now, even more, and you'll never read this second letter, maybe you'll never read anything of mine ever again. But all the same, there will always be the hope that you'll return in, who knows, a whole week, or even months, years, to the envelope you'd forgotten, tossed away some-where, weeks, months, years, until, who knows, one day, a careless lapse, a slip, an unthinking moment, and this letter will be opened, and all the world that it contains will open, too. It was saying to you the whole time: Remember? And even if I'm wrong, and you throw them away, one after another, resolved, unforgiving, throw away this one and those still to come. Yes, because there will be others. How many? I don't know yet. But there will be others, every day, in your mailbox, every day, waiting for you, the envelope closed with all its possibilities. Then even if you throw them away, one after another, there will always be another closed envelope and the expectation of the closed envelope's own language.

But I'd rather imagine that things aren't like that. I prefer something much simpler: you as you are now, sitting in an armchair, or on a dining chair at the table, or on the sofa, with this letter and a cup of coffee. The phone ringing. Your hands and this letter. Only this. The minimum necessary. I've always thought it's necessary to be uncomplicated when there is something important to say. Is there really something important to say? you must be asking yourself. A revelation, a secret? I answer yes, there are things you don't know, there are always things one doesn't know, however transparent the other person might be. However quiet, there is always something unexpected, something that might surprise you, and make you smile or suffer.

A small revenge. What is revenge, after all, but a strange declaration of love, somebody taking revenge is always somebody who's saying: Separation, separation is a half-finished gesture and your name is repeated over again. Your name, unfinished, suspended in my mouth, that's revenge, a love that never ends.

So that was what happened, a small revenge, yesterday. I'm saying it was yesterday, but it could have been earlier, any other day following your absence, and so I'm saying, because I'm the one telling the story: yesterday I went back to the rental place. I tell you this almost in secret, fearfully perhaps. I went to the rental place for the first time since that day; there was the same door, the same movies, the same man behind the counter, but something had changed, something in me. I picked up that exact same movie from last time, remember? The one I suggested—was I trying to tell you something? But you didn't want to see; you grabbed my arm so hard the pressure of your fingers lingered for a long time. That movie, that character, the actor who does or doesn't look like you. But it's all the same now, and I got the movie. Was that cruel? Perhaps. And it was like I was betraying you—that's strange, isn't it? It was like I was deceiving you, like I was taking revenge, or worse, like I was taking revenge and smiling about it. See how everything's changed? I felt happy, a disturbance, an excitement; I was practically running, glowing, in the middle of the street, feeling like I'd stolen something valuable and was getting away without anybody noticing, unharmed. And I was smiling, glowing, for no reason at all.

I could tell you that when I arrived home, I put the movie in the machine. I pressed Play, and out came a whole unfurling of scenes with that actor and that character, everything you wouldn't acknowledge, which could have been you. And I could say that I spent that whole time in front of the television feeling happy at all those things that would have made you smile and suffer. I could say all this—but no. I could even lie—but no. For some reason, the movie alone awoke the sense of some danger, an unspecified fear. So I put the disc back in the case, closed it, and there it stayed for a long time on top of the table, while I sat in front of the empty noise from the television, the television devoid of images. My small act of revenge, infantile and foolish. I could lie. But no. Because revenge is never enough, like love. What's the difference?

All that nonsense of going to the rental place to pick up the movie was only the start of the things I didn't do, and which I could do to hurt you, to wound you. I could confirm so many things, things you're afraid of, couldn't I? I could tell you, for example, every detail, every minute detail, of the clothes I was wearing—that red dress, remember? You always liked seeing me in red, it looked so good on me, the dress that left my back bare, the dark red dress, carmine red, my back bare, my black hair untied, which you used to compare to a dark curtain, like night? I could tell you all the details about that red dress, the untied hair, the way you liked me to wear it, isn't that how it was? And I could, for example, tell you I washed my hair with the finest essences, the finest oils, spent long hours in front of the mirror. I put my makeup on carefully, my body still damp, perfumed myself all over, as though going on a date, as though for a lover, my body gentle and precise. Then I put on the sandals with the straps, the ones with the extremely high heels, the ones that after a few hours make my feet and legs hurt horribly and that I only wore to please you, remember? I would do anything to please you. The sandals you liked so much because you knew what discomfort they caused me, the straps squeezing my toes and the heels on which I struggled to keep my balance. And so I tell you all this, my body perfumed, the dress, the makeup, the sandals wobbling around the house, the noise of my footsteps on the floorboards when you arrived and I went to let you in, the noise of my footsteps and my nervous breathing until I got to the door and opened the door and saw you, smiling, as though all of it were obvious, the fact that I should be getting myself ready for you. But this time I wasn't walking toward the door and you weren't waiting for me and thinking it obvious; there was only me and the carmine-red dress and the movie on the living room table, the movie I didn't fully watch but its existence, its presence, was enough to mean something. A small act of revenge, a confidence, because the other person, however submissive, however transparent, always has something unexpected within them, something that might make you smile or suffer.

I could tell you about all that preparation, the dress, the perfume, the movie I didn't watch and everything that didn't happen afterward. Yes, because it wasn't only the movie. It wasn't just the movie, that small revenge, infantile and foolish, but everything that came afterward, that moment that never should have existed. So I'm telling you that contrary to what you might be imagining, I didn't go out afterward. No, I didn't go out or walk from bar to bar, along the streets, through the darkest places in the city. No, I didn't offer myself up, ready and perfumed, a new smile, an invitation. No, I didn't wrap myself around other bodies, didn't smell other perfumes, didn't kiss other mouths, nor did I bring my face close to another face, to the roughness of another face. This is how it was. I didn't run down the stairs, or dance, or sing or shout that none of it mattered, I didn't smile at other lips, or approach other men, or feel desire, or allow others to desire me, obedient, happy, no, I didn't run my fingers over another skin, the tips of my fingers, nor the softness of my skin over another skin, I did none of this. I didn't dance all night, the day dawning in other mouths, no, I didn't wake up in other beds, or in my own bed with sheets wrapping around other bodies, rumpled sheets, no, I didn't condemn you, nor did I turn my back on you and smile, among other lives, other breaths, no, I didn't feel the weight of another body, of another hand, or a different rhythm of breathing on the back of my neck, no, I didn't cry or suffer in other arms, I didn't open my body to other eyes, other revelations, nor did I undress nervously in the middle of the living room or beside another bed, no, I didn't take off my red dress, or any item of clothing that you liked, just for you, for someone else, didn't untie my hair the way you preferred it, for someone else, or feel the caress of other words in my ear, no, I did none of this. I didn't run down the stairs, or through any dark corner of the city, I didn't smile at the first stranger, didn't offer myself up with my gaze alight or walk listlessly in the opposite direction, no, I didn't allow other hands on my skin, which you said was so soft, other hands and another voice talking about the softness of my skin and the curtain of my hair, no other voice wrapping itself around mine, another caress, no, I did none of this, all the small revenges I might have taken, and writing to you now, and making you smile or suffer. But no. I did none of this. I just closed my eyes and sat here.

So why all this? you might be thinking. This laying out of what I did not do, this inventory of revenges aborted. A very subtle kind of punishment? A declaration of love? I don't know, maybe just a declaration of weakness to make you smile or suffer, or maybe a way of wanting you, of reaching you, to establish a link between us, an impossible link, which I established only because I'm here, because there's this distance between what I write and what you read, because it's been days since I've washed, since I've combed my hair, since I've left the house.

A.

I I

The mirror reflected the image of a man who was still young, in spite of some early wrinkles and hair and a beard that were turning white unexpectedly fast, and a three-year-old girl sitting on a stool. His daughter, he reminded himself, which was the way his thoughts tended to go lately when the girl was at home, his weekend thoughts since the separation. Standing in front of the mirror he was trying with an unpracticed hand to comb the girl's long, curly red hair. From time to time she would complain, but on the whole she allowed herself to be combed, with a serious expression on her face, slightly smug, as though she felt sorry for her father, as though she understood the massive effort required to comb the hair of a three-year-old girl.

Though this did not signify any clemency, any forgiveness, and nor did it mean she was inclined to make his job any easier. On the contrary, she stayed just where she was, unmoving, posing like a princess faced with a lowly subject. He felt incapable; something about her intimidated him. He had felt that way ever since the beginning, when she was just a dislocated baby placed into his arms in the maternity ward.

He held the baby for the first time one day after the birth; as his ex-wife liked to recall, he was the only man who'd managed to take twenty-four hours to get to the hospital, which was only ten minutes away from home. He had never been able to explain what had happened. The truth was, he couldn't remember; he couldn't remember, he had told his wife. She hadn't said as much, but it was clear she would never forgive him. And she never did. Women can be terribly resentful, that was his conclusion. He arranged the curls as best he could on the girl's shoulders.

"All set, Manuela, now we've just got to wait for your mother."

"Dad!"

The girl held up a pink hair clip toward her father's reflection in the mirror.

"You forgot."

Right, he'd forgotten. He took the clip, examined how it

worked. He pulled a lock of hair and arranged it in such a way that it wouldn't fall into her face.

"Yeah, you're right, it's good now. You're even more beautiful than before," he said, forcing a smile, trying to start a conversation.

The girl showed no trace of any response; she jumped down from the stool and went off to play in her room. A princess, he thought. Haughty and arrogant. He'd talk to his ex-wife as soon as she arrived; she was spoiling the girl.

His ex-wife arrived with two rings of the doorbell announcing that it was her, one of those things that never changes. He got up off the sofa and went to open the door. She came in as though, instead of just her, there were a whole army entering the apartment, a crowd behind her, her perfume spreading through the rooms; every space felt immediately occupied by her. She kissed him on both cheeks.

"Hi, Marcos—you okay?"

"Hi, Marcos"—he'd never get used to his ex-wife calling him that, someone who for so long had called him "my sweet," "my love." She sounded so distracted now, so uninterested— "Oh, hi, Marcos"—he'd lived with the woman for years, they'd had a child together, a house, a joint account, a life, and one day all of it stopped existing and she became just a perfumed stranger who walked through the door and said, as she might say to anybody, "Hi, Marcos."

"Yeah, okay."

His ex-wife paid no attention to his answer, she was looking severely over the disorder of the apartment, the moving crates scattered around the living room, the few pieces of furniture he'd bought, a parched plant he always forgot to water.

"Why don't you clean up this mess? It's been more than a month since you moved."

He gave a distracted reply, as though her advice were aimed at someone else:

"I will, I'm going to tidy up, as soon as I get a bit of time."

"Everyone's got time, you've just got to want to do it."

He pretended not to have heard. She smiled and changed the subject.

"And what about Manu, where's she?"

His ex-wife loved calling the girl Manu. They'd argued about this countless times; they'd chosen Manuela, so why would you then call her Manu, Lulu, Bilu, or whatever else? What a ridiculous compulsion of her mother's to ruin the lovely name, Manuela, by calling the girl by some nickname or other.

"Manuela's in her bedroom."

"Manu, darling!"

The girl came running to her mother, it was like they'd been parted for centuries, separated against their will. And now right before his eyes, they celebrated their reunion, so fervently longed for by them both.

"How are you, my love? Tell Mommy."

And he just stood there, in the doorway, watching that moment. The two of them embracing, the girl with an affection, a passion, she would never show him. And he just stood there, imagining himself as an ogre or something.

"Want a drink?"

"No, thanks, I don't have time. We still have to go by my mother's."

"Yes, of course, your mother. How's she doing?"

"She's fine, though her arthritis is still a problem, as you know."

"Yeah, I know."

"And what about the two of you? How was the weekend? Did she eat properly?"

The girl looked tired in her mother's arms, her arms around her mother's neck, as though she'd had a long wait, had been through an ordeal.

"It was great, Manuela drew several versions of Felipe, then we went out for a pizza. This morning we played a little game on the computer."

His ex-wife put the girl down on the floor.

"Go on, sweetheart, go get your teddy, we've got to go to Grandma's."

The girl obeyed at once, he noticed. In two minutes she was back with the pink teddy bear. The girl held her mother's hand.

This was the woman he had met when she was still very young. Both of them had trained as architects. She was now an interior designer, a famous interior designer who was booked to work on the most sought-after houses in the city. A dynamic woman, always had been; well connected, always had been. As for him, he was neither dynamic nor well connected. He'd never ended up working in architecture. Life had taken its own course. But it was all still pretty good, he had no cause to complain. He handed over the backpack with the girl's things.

"Thank you. Well, we'll head off, you understand, my mother's waiting."

"Of course."

"Manu, love, give your dad a kiss."

The girl hesitated, but at her mother's insistent stare she approached him. He crouched down for her to press her mouth quickly to his cheek.

"You ought to shave," his ex-wife remarked as she said goodbye.

"I will," he said automatically.

And there he stood with the door open, as they waited for the elevator. Mother and daughter, and later they would be meeting the grandmother. A kind of female clan, with a matriarchal lineage, a bond that united them and made them mysterious, inaccessible—he just stood there, forever excluded from their pact. He remembered a photograph his ex-wife had put on the coffee table in the living room, the three of them, grandmother, mother and daughter: the grandmother, a very elegant woman sitting in an armchair, her granddaughter on her lap, her daughter crouching down to be at their height. He would often sit in the living room and look at that photo. His mother-in-law, with whom he had a relationship that was polite though dry, his wife, who was increasingly a stranger, and his daughter, this girl who was so very distant. He looked at the two of them in the hallway, both silent; maybe those few minutes' wait was making them uncomfortable. He felt uncomfortable, too. And when the elevator arrived, at last they could say goodbye.

"Bye, Marcos."

"Bye." He could barely hear his own voice.

As he closed the door, he felt both relief and sadness. It was almost as though his wife, his daughter and that whole line of women had ceased to exist. And he realized that he had longed all day for that moment, when the door closed and he was at last alone at home. Finally the time and the space he needed. The letter. The thought that had not manifested itself—buried by the presence of his daughter and by everything that presence signified—but which had somehow been with him, discreet, asleep but insistent, the whole day.

He went into the kitchen and poured himself a cup of coffee. He returned to the living room, put the cup down on the table, picked up the blue envelope he had left there that morning, slightly hidden under electricity and gas bills. This time he had opened the envelope right away while still in the elevator, without the reluctance he had felt the previous day. Something was propelling him forward, impatience, curiosity. He looked at the letter carefully, the same handwriting, the same name, his address. In place of the sender's name, just an initial. The fountain pen. That rounded handwriting. The envelope opened easily, opened in a kind of desperate longing. He noticed now that this time it didn't have a stamp, a detail he hadn't spotted that morning; it caught his breath for a few moments, the idea that she might be there, so close. That she might have dropped off the letter herself. He went over to the window, as though expecting to see her. Her quick, careful steps. Perhaps a shadow coming into the building, the long black hair, the red dress, her back naked, the envelope between her fingers. The address she believed to be her lover's but that was now his, the apartment where he lived now, the moving crates still scattered around the living room, the view from the window. Could it be that, at some point, she had leaned right where he was leaning now on the windowsill, her eyes on the same sight he was looking at, the same landscape? He thought, Is that how it was?

My darling,

I ended up returning the movie without watching it. I went by the rental place and returned it, not making a big scene. Why am I telling you this? I don't know, perhaps to please you, to redeem myself. To redeem myself for some unexpected mistake, something that might happen by accident, those things that are impossible to control. And at the same time for things that had always been planned, the worst crimes, the worst plots. To confess something, not even just to please you; I would do anything to please you. However, even if I'm spending my days thinking about everything I say to you and about the effect of my words, will anything change? Will I in any way be a part of your life, or just the contrary, will we move further apart? Because it's always possible to be further apart. Could there be some limit, a border to halt the process of distancing? Could there be a maximum distance between us, or is it something that continues to expand, uninterrupted, as time passes? At first, absence is everything that absence means: pain, joy and, who knows, even fatigue, then only a name, an image, then one day not even that, just a suspicion, an empty space.

And once more I wonder what you might be asking yourself, what's this whole thing for, after all? Maybe you ask this with each letter. Without really understanding the reason for these interrogations and memories and strategies. Why all this going round and round? You sit there, on the sofa, in the armchair, holding this letter and you're irritated at my lack of concision. So I will be clear. I will answer you, without any circumlocutions this time, without repetitions, simply and without a big scene, which is the way the most extraordinary things really happen, important things: I'm writing for you to read me. Simple as that. For you to read me and turn back to me again, for you to read my words and think that there is something surprisingly beautiful inside me, something you hadn't seen, something we'd never noticed. And so, to be even clearer—is that possible?—for you to read me and love me. Why not? Someone else reading these letters might love me, don't you think? Even if loving isn't as easy as all that—you're probably thinking, Love isn't as easy as all that. When you're no longer in love, after love has appeared and lived and died and turned into something like a plant or any other organic matter, you think, Love isn't some organic matter; love is something else. It won't turn into a seed, you say, that's not all organic matter is, gardening, working the soil, love isn't a seed to turn into a plant and water and all those silly things that people like to think when they're happy, this happiness that's silly in the way all happinesses are, that makes us think it's possible to recover the unrecoverable. You say all this now, as you read this letter, or maybe you've already said it or thought it about the previous letter, but I go on and I argue, insisting again, that there is something surprisingly beautiful inside me.

I was thinking about this yesterday, about love, about this insistence on love, as though love could save us from everything, as though love could save us from hate, from madness and even desire. Whoever came up with that idea? Love can't even save us from love.

What can be said, then, about sadness, about indifference, and that inevitable moment when love ends?

That moment we think will never come. And how are we to know when love ends? Will there be a moment, a dividing line, a revelation, an internal alarm clock that goes off, then right when we wake up, we say, sleepily, Right, it's over. We get up, we get dressed, take our bag or suitcase and leave. Outside, the morning light of another day, people on the buses going to work, children in uniform, coffee with milk at the bakeries, all so everyday, so normal. How can it all be so normal, while inside an apartment, in a bedroom, in a bed, is love that has just ended.

Or does love start ending right from the beginning, from the first kiss, the first look, the sense that something is being worn down, dissolving away. And however many kisses and gazes, and all the happy, foolish words we can invent, there's always a lurking something that troubles us. Something that, at the precise moment when it starts, also sets in motion the inevitable process of extinction.

Why all this? All these words about love, that can only be obvious and foolish, it's true. My answer is that it's just a way for me to get closer. To get closer, carefully, to what really matters. Why do stories end without ever revealing what happens afterward, what happens after the story ends? Isn't that where the most important thing is, aren't we missing something?

At what point might we draw the line that separated us? You could even argue that we were separated from the start. But I'd rather not. I'd rather there be an event, an act, a moment when we got up and said, Right, it's over. And what if it wasn't us, that plural that includes us both in a single act, in drawn-out synchronized gestures, and what if it wasn't us, but only you, who one day woke up, got out of bed and said, as though you'd heard an internal alarm clock only you could hear, the ringing of an alarm clock only you could hear, said, Right, it's over. This single fact would be the beginning of countless little movements, which I would have no way of following, as I lay there, out of sync, thinking about the previous night and about everything that had happened and the way that you suddenly, without looking at me, without saying a single word, got up and put your clothes on and left. How was it possible that, from one moment to the next, you could wake up, get out of bed and leave. How could it be so simple? I couldn't understand, and just went on lying there.

I remember that you woke up, or perhaps you'd been awake all night; I was awake all night, hating you deeply, have I told you that? I spent the whole night hating you deeply; it's so foolish and vulgar, hatred. But that's how it was, foolish and vulgar, and I hated you and at the same time wanted to hug you tight as though trying to reassure myself, at every moment, that you were still there next to me. In the middle of the night I was hugging you, how is that possible? You were in bed with your back to me—how could I be hugging you, after everything? But I was hugging you, my arm around your chest, a hug that was gentle and firm, because I sensed that there was something getting away from me. It's always possible to lose what you don't have, it's always possible to move further away, the unlimited possibility of loss. I sensed this and much more, because deep down we always sense these things. In the middle of all this I told you I was just lying there, but it's not true, I was lying there and there was extreme rage and resentment and a desire that you should leave, and, at the same time, the fear of your leaving, of your finally getting up and leaving. The whole night, my arm was around you in your unmoving sleep, as if I didn't exist. I stayed there, the whole night as if I didn't exist, my arm cinched tight around your chest in an attempt to prevent that last link from coming apart. I should have sent you away the moment you approached silently, lay down on my bed, as though I weren't a part of it, lay down on my bed, turned onto your side and fell asleep, saying nothing to me. How could you have slept, just like that, so simply? As if nothing had happened—how can somebody sleep like that? I should have sent you away, from the first moment, but no. For some reason. The whole night spent with your back to me, and me hugging you in that last link of ours. Awake. All night long.

But then the day broke, because every day it breaks, the first rays of sun on the bed and the remains of the night in the bed. You got up in silence, always silence, since the day before, since our trip to the rental place and the night that came after. I should have sent you away, I should have hated you and sent you away. But no. I just lay there, under the sheet, clinging to the sheet the same way I had wrapped around your body not long before, I clung to the sheet with a hug, a kind of salvation, even knowing that it was just a sheet, as unanchored as me, a sheet that can't even be a plank of wood, or a rope.

You got up in silence, put on your clothes, picked up the backpack that you'd left on the floor and I'd put on the chair. And now I think about these little details, after everything, that day and that night, and after what came later. After everything, I'd seen your backpack open on the floor of the bedroom, and I had closed it and put it on the chair—how is that possible, I think now, I should have thrown it in the trash, should have burned it, something to destroy you, however small, but no. I took such care, an automatic gesture, such care.

But now I'm lost, where was I? Your backpack. Yes, you got up, put on your clothes, picked up your backpack and left. I remember my reaction when I saw you leaving the room. After everything, you simply picked up your things and left, just like that, saying nothing, no goodbyes, no explanations. At the time I thought I would never have such strength, such resentment, such a terrible desire to do you harm, to get to you, make you suffer. And at that moment I might have been capable of anything, anything that hurt, anything excruciating. I might have been capable of the most extraordinary things.

You got up, put on your clothes and left. I clung to the sheet, which I was now dragging across the bed, across the bedroom floor, and I followed you, asking something, but you left in silence and I called to you, following you to the door, the sheet dragging along the floor of the hallway, of the dining room. I was wrapped up in the sheet, like a bride, a sheet dragging along the hallway, through the dining room, like a naked bride and with all the expectation of a bride, begging you to love me, to say something, or even if you didn't love me to stay, even when you stood at the door, your hand turning the door handle in a movement that seemed to go on forever. And now, as I write to you and think of that image, that last image, your hand turning the door handle and me behind you, I see at once that I'm trying to give all this a more dramatic color than it had in reality, even in slightly poor taste, perhaps, like a bride, honestly, what could be more dramatic and tasteless, but I also think, Isn't that how goodbyes ought to be? Me behind you, wrapped in the sheet, like a ghostly bride begging something of you, isn't that how suffering ought to be, pathetic, dramatic, in extremely poor taste? Isn't that how anything extreme ought to be?

But it was not, as you know. The moment when things happen never takes on the importance it should. Only much later, when time has passed and life has passed and everything has passed. In the moment, it's the opposite, it's all so quick, so simple, without making a scene, which is how the most extraordinary things happen.

Then you got up, put on your clothes, picked up your backpack and left. There. Simple. Without looking at me, or addressing a word to me. And I stayed there, lying in bed. Looking at your body and your movements that were now so unreal, so distant, movements that were unknown. I stayed there, unmoving, silent, looking at your body and then at the absence of your body, at the space created that had been occupied by the thing that once was you and the space you occupied, in my room, in my bed. I didn't say anything, I didn't cry, didn't ask for explanations, didn't beg you not to go. I just stayed there, unmoving, silent, lying on the bed, while you put on your clothes, picked up your backpack and left.

A.

III

A recently separated man needs a woman who has at least a minimal amount of understanding. A woman to be with him at times when he's most sociable, and who will leave him alone when solitude becomes indispensable again. But women understand only what matters to them, he thought as he hung up the phone. And the need to cancel their plans for that day was something Fabiane wasn't remotely interested in understanding. Her response was to make the most wide-ranging recriminations. It was the second time he'd canceled on her, it's true, but tomorrow, tomorrow night, without fail, he'd said on the phone. She had accepted after a protracted reluctance.

"Fine, tomorrow night, but if you cancel one more time, just one, I swear it's over. If there still really is anything between us."

"I won't cancel, I promise, today really was something unexpected that came up."

"Right, and Saturday, too, looks like your life is full of unexpected things just coming up."

"No, Saturday it was because Manuela had the flu, there was no way I could have taken her, I've explained that already."

"Right, and so now you're using your daughter as your excuse for everything."

Beautiful women tend to be more complicated, perhaps because their beauty has made things too easy for them, given them a lot of options and little need to face reality. Beautiful women tend to be self-centered and childish, he thought, they never escape from the role of little princess and expect that the man, as their subject, or as a father who will deny them nothing, is going to spoil them and demand nothing in return, just because they are beautiful. Fabiane, he thought, was an extremely beautiful woman.

After he hung up, he gathered the papers on the desk, picked up his things and went out. He had decided to leave work early that day. Not because he had any particularly pressing commitment, which was what he had told Fabiane, but just the need to be alone, to go for a walk after the long weekend with the girl, after seeing his ex-wife—he was exhausted, despite having done nothing. He had used what was left of Sunday just to walk around the apartment with no clear objective in mind. And now, the whole day he had been unable to concentrate, all that paperwork on the desk awaiting his attention, the e-mails, the phone calls he hadn't made to people who had rung him, only Fabiane, the crucial call just to cancel. He wouldn't be in the mood to meet up for dinner, to drink, to listen to Fabiane's endless conversation, her complaints, troubles with the boss, troubles with her mother, troubles with her sister, in short, Fabiane's troubles. She wanted to change everything, she'd say, a different life. She'd say the life she had was nothing like what she'd dreamed of—she wanted to leave her job, have a life that was calmer, children. Fabiane wanted two children, a happy marriage, a nicely decorated apartment, a husband well set up financially. He had commented, just to warn her, that he had a daughter already, that he had no intention of having more, that he was very far from being a good parent, besides which he'd just gotten separated, the whole thing was really stressful, he'd been looking for an apartment, moving, establishing a new routine. She looked at him angrily, got to her feet, annoyed, and left in a fury. Was that what he got for being honest? Honesty never did anyone any good, he thought. He'd been right to cancel, better that way, a bit of peace and quiet for the night.

On the way home he thought of stopping by the rental place. It hadn't been even a month since he'd moved and he didn't yet know the neighborhood shops very well, but he remembered the rental place nearby that he'd seen the other day, when he had strayed from his usual routine in search of a drugstore. Manuela only used a particular kind of sunblock that was especially for three-year-olds. His ex-wife insisted he use that one, she'd called and told him so first thing in the morning. But sunblock is all the same, he replied, already getting ready to take the girl to the beach, and if the one I've got works on me, why wouldn't it work on her? He'd tried to argue, but his ex-wife was tenacious. He could have not bought it, could have just pretended; the girl, however, gave him a penetrating look, she knew his lies, all his little tricks, he thought. A three-year-old child understands everything. And before they went to the beach, the two of them sought out a drugstore together. He was thinking that the separation had only caused more trouble for him—the girl, who had previously been her mother's responsibility, at least as far as everyday matters were concerned, to whom he just gave the odd affectionate caress when he got home from the office, had now become a visible, insistent being in his life. If it had been up to him, he

wouldn't have separated, he thought, not because his relationship with his ex-wife was a good one (it hadn't been for
years, not since the pregnancy), but he had never thought of
separating, maybe because he felt guilty, yes, because it had
been he who'd become more distant, ever since the pregnancy. Now his daughter was his on weekends, he was on
his own with the task of distracting a child.

Before the separation everything had seemed easier, and
even if it didn't make him happy, even if he had sometimes
felt like leaving, he had never given it any serious thought,
there was always something preventing him. Until the moment when his wife said it was over. What's over, he asked,
not entirely understanding. The marriage, love, everything,
she said. Everything had been over for some time. He kept
looking at her, trying to understand, how was this possible,
how was it possible that things should be over just like that,
from one moment to the next? After all, they had a house, a
life, a daughter. But his wife would not be intimidated, she
looked at him with contempt, and he was the one who'd had
to leave. So that's how it was, from one day to the next, his
wife decided it was over and he was the one who'd had to
leave, leave everything, find someplace new to live as quickly
as possible, she insisted on it as she strode about the living
room. That same woman who not long before had said
she loved him, hadn't she? Recollections muddled in his

memory. He even asked if she had someone else, but no, she said no, she said she was just tired, tired of him, that he never did anything for anyone, tired of his selfishness, of his absence, she said all this and many other things, the things women say when they're angry.

He said nothing, just took his belongings and moved to the guest room, then to the new apartment. A small apartment, but with a nice view of the mountain, the first one he found (the truth was he didn't have the patience to go on looking). He moved right away, bought a few pieces of furniture, just the essentials. And he realized then that there was no going back. He went to collect the remainder of his things from his house, his ex-house. His ex-wife was waiting for him with everything already packed up, labeled, she had always been so perfect, so efficient, even in this. He could have fought with her, but he didn't feel he had the energy for what would probably end up being an endless argument, with his wife saying the blame lay with him, that he'd ruined her life and their child's. Women can be extremely cruel when they want to be. He took his things and left. He considered asking after Manuela, where she was, since she hadn't come to say goodbye to her father, but he ended up not asking anything. His ex-wife, who seemed able to read his thoughts, remarked: Don't worry, Manu can spend weekends with you, it'll be good for her, for both of you. She said this before she closed the door and disappeared.

Things happened without his having any control, he thought. There was always someone deciding things for him. The wedding had been an idea of his ex-wife's—she'd so insisted that he ended up accepting; then the child, without a question or a warning. Did he by any chance want one, did he even agree? No, nothing, she'd just gotten herself pregnant. The need for a new job, all those changes, then the separation. This was what the last few years had been like, an unfurling of things happening against his wishes.

But it would be different from now on, he thought, as he drove to the rental place. It had been months since he'd watched a movie, since he'd been to the movie theater. He had woken up that morning with this thought, and felt something had changed without his noticing, and he felt glad that he had canceled his date, that he was on his way to the rental place instead, that he had the evening and all night ahead of him. Everything awaited him. Something so simple.

The place was empty. He registered as a member, gave his new address, the phone number he didn't yet know by heart, he listed his ex-wife as his emergency contact, one of those automatic responses. Then he crossed her name out. Emergency contact: NONE, he wrote in capital letters. He wanted to say it aloud, right there, none. But he said nothing. He handed the form to the attendant and went to look for a movie. He looked carefully at the cases, one by one, paying no attention to the title or the director, as though he were looking for something specific, something very important; the attendant came over to him, and asked:

"Are you looking for any movie in particular, sir?"

He gave a start, quickly put the case he was holding back on the shelf. He replied very quietly, practically a murmur:

"Right, I am, yes, I mean, no, not something in particular, I'm just browsing."

"If you need any help, just ask."

"Of course, I will, yes, thank you."

It bothered him, first that he'd been called "sir"—he was, after all, still a young man—and second that he'd been offered help. It was an unwanted approach. He went on looking, not completely sure what he was looking for, or why he was there. He went past the horror section, the adventure section, and focused on the comedies, then the dramas. He examined each cover quickly, one by one, and put it back in its place. He felt the attendant watching him curiously from behind the counter; he avoided catching his eye so as not to be asked any more questions. He ended up choosing five movies, which had nothing in common but the photo on the cover: always a young man with strong features and a blond actress. He paid for them and left as quickly as he could, his head down as though running away, as though afraid that someone would discover a secret even he didn't know.

On the drive back home, the happiness from going to the rental place was replaced by a certain anxiety, that everything had become urgent. A fear that things might fly out of his control once again. He tried to calm down. When he reached his building, he drove in, still hurrying, parked the car and went straight to the mailbox, opened it tentatively, a few moments of fear that he might be mistaken, then immediately the feeling of relief—no, the letter was there. He took his correspondence and put it all in the bag with the movies, pushed the button for the elevator. A few other people stood waiting next to him; with a nod he greeted the neighbor he'd chatted with before. As he waited, with the movies and mail in his bag, he felt revived, happy to have the whole night ahead of him, without any obstacles, just him. First he'd look at the mail, he thought, trying to give this idea an air of indifference, of mere accident, then he'd turn on the TV and watch a movie, any one of them. But he was lying, there was no indifference, no mere accident. Once in the elevator, standing in silence, he realized that for the first time in a long while, something was really touching him, reaching him.

JANUARY 22

My darling,

The day dawned cloudy, a summer's day but strangely cold and humid, a humidity that got right into your bones. I slept and woke up freezing to death, the duvet had fallen off the side of the bed, and I had been freezing the whole night but not enough to wake up. I woke up late this morning, dragged myself to the bathroom, turned on the water and looked at myself in the mirror, my face increasingly unrecognizable in the reflection. I took a shower, standing in the hot water. I'd give anything to have a bathtub—you know that, how many times have I told you I'd give anything for a bathtub to lie in for hours and hours in the hot water—have I told you that before? All the pleasure of soaking in hot water. I always think about people who die like that, in the bath. It's a romantic death, don't you think? Not the business of slitting your wrists, which seems an appalling violence, and I'm someone who's always been so afraid of violence, as you know, right? So not slitting wrists, then, with all that blood, the blood, I was always so scared of blood, there are people who faint at the sight of it, streaming out of the body, flowing, why should that be? Perhaps because it's an emblem, a sign, a sign that there's something inside the body, something living and pulsing and streaming, a whole independent life inside the body, a secret life, like a foreign body.

Maybe that's the reason for the shock, as we imagine ourselves hollow, but no, we imagine ourselves clean, but no. Inside us there's this whole heap of cells and tissues and organs. I remember my biology class where we learned that fat inside our bodies is yellow, and we grimaced in disgust, pounds and pounds of a kind of tissue, a yellow sponge. Some people considered this receptacle of stored-up energy sacred, did you know that? But that wasn't something I learned in biology class; I only learned that much later.

In biology class we learned that blood is blue. Blood inside our bodies is blue, did you know that? And it only acquires that red tinge when in contact with oxygen in the atmosphere. We only see blue blood when we take a close look at our veins, hidden behind a veil of skin and arteries, the blue blood that gets away from us, that we can only imagine. There's something mysterious inside our bodies, don't you think? And violence, violence is nothing more than an approach toward this mystery, this unimaginable thing contained inside of us. Perhaps a criminal, a murderer, an assassin, is simply somebody who's fascinated, someone who doubts, someone who does not conform, someone who like a child, with no thought for the consequences, opens up the belly of a frog to see that mystery inside the frog, pulsating, that something that draws your gaze if it moves and suffers and feels hunger and fear. Like a surgeon with his gloves and his sterilized instruments, a surgeon who draws a long cut down the body, just to see that thing pulsing inside, and is like the criminal and the assassin. The body opened up and the pain that goes with it. Will the mystery inside appear along with the pain? The physical pain we inflict on another, from the subtlest to the most unbearable, might physical pain be a kind of revelation? A kind of being alive, a kind of pleasure? Might physical pain be a kind of religiosity? A very profound kind of love? The love of someone who surrenders their body to the greatest acts of violence, the greatest atrocities, someone who leaves themselves open, soft, submissive on any surface, on the surgeon's table, on a bed, on an altar?

And could there be any greater violence than entering another person's body—a dagger, a bullet, any tool that penetrates someone else's body, any arrow, any organ. How is it possible to enter someone else's body, just like that, with impunity? To introduce any organ into another person's body, isn't that a kind of extinction? And then, having been in someone else's body, wrapped in the most hidden tissues, the most secret tissues in another person's body, and to reemerge covered in smells and mucus and wetness, covered in the most absolute intimacy, how is it possible to come out so completely unharmed, free, and then just roll over and close your eyes and fall asleep, as though nothing had happened, this extreme violence, how is it possible to wake up the following day, get dressed and leave, I ask you. How is it possible to leave while the other person is still lying there, on the surgeon's table, on the bed, on the altar, the other person lying there, unmoving, exposed, defenseless. The other person with their marks and their bruises and their pains, with violence and love and the pleasure of violence and love engraved there forever, the other person with their body opened up, and the window, and the sun and the morning light, while out in the world, people are buying their newspapers and children are wearing their school uniforms and the day is unfolding.

Because you know, you know what I'm talking about. Even if I don't say it, you always know what I'm talking about. Because we do know, because there's an invisible link uniting us. Like a piece of music, the piece of music that was playing that day, remember? When you looked at me and laughed and ran your fingers down my face. At that exact moment, that piece of music was playing and our laughter, our movements, the music was infused in our memory with that love, remember? Because afterward, afterward, even if time has passed and I have passed and you have passed, even if, afterward, anytime that piece of music happens to be playing anywhere, a party, a movie, a train station, we'll remember that music and everything it meant. Remember?

I remember everything, ever since the first day, the first look. Somebody once told me that everything's contained in that first look: the love, meeting, meeting again, separation, pleasure, pain, life and hatred. Everything that is yet to come exists already in that first look.

Everything that comes after is not like in a movie, or like some mystical knowledge, not like an oracle, but just a logical succession of facts and certainties, each linking onto the next. And so in that first look I knew everything that would follow, everything that would happen when love rose up and stretched out and ended. How did I know? Perhaps because it was all mine, because I had carried that moment with me, always, that possibility.

Like all of us, our lives unfold with the tedium of the everyday and of the obvious things of the everyday: waking, sleeping, working, eating, loving, hearing, forgiving, shopping, always safe, everything always so gentle and slow and sad, the life we construct with such fragility, ordinary life, the life it's tolerable to live, but along with that there's always this shadow, this imbalance, this possibility. Chaos is always lying in wait for us, at any moment, because we are the ones who bear it, always waiting, the secret hope that something is finally going to happen, that something is going to happen and propel us toward what we longed for, what we feared, what we never had the courage to name. The first look is merely the confirmation, a reflection in the bathroom in the morning, the first look is a mirror in which we see ourselves for the first time, unrecognizable, and in wonder we notice something that's incredibly beautiful in ourselves. Do you understand? I'm finding it hard, too, but I'm trying to explain it to you. But what for, you'll say? So that you will love me? Perhaps.

Do you remember the first time we met? I came over and said something to you, what was it I said again? Odd, I don't remember. What could it have been, that first line, what was that first question of mine? And what did you answer, I don't remember, odd, isn't it? That I should remember the look and everything within it, and have forgotten the rest: my question, your answer, what you were wearing, were you smoking, were you smiling, were you drinking or was the glass in your hand empty? I don't know. Why should it be that we always forget what's most important? But I do know that we talked and that at a certain point you asked whether I might want you to walk me home. Was that it? Or were those my words? I no longer know, but I remember you coming up with me in the elevator, I remember opening the front door and looking at the living room and the furniture in the living room and thinking I was entering for the first time, as though all of it, the house, the furniture, me myself, as though all of it were strange and new to me. I offered you a drink, right? You were smiling,

I remember you were smiling and I wondered what that smile of yours meant, what you were thinking, and I would have given anything to know what you were thinking. And I still felt strange, as though I were the guest. As though I were in my house for the first time.

What followed was more or less as might be expected, do you remember? To begin with, at least. I remember that your body began moving delicately onto mine, your hand in my hair, on my back, very delicately on my back, your kisses, gentle, your words of affection, of kindness. You moved closer, carefully. To begin with. An encounter like any other. Then, from one moment to the next, there was a transformation in your movements, a shock, a return to something more ancient, something that was always there between us, and that we were now recognizing in each other, and your rhythm was different now and your touch was different now. Your hand, incisive now, your hand, palm flat, your hand closing on mine, your mouth, my mouth losing itself in yours, and in the words from your mouth, the words that were beautiful, obscene and frightening from your mouth. You were all strength and will, you were a bestial stranger, something much more ancient, and wrapped around me in a greedy embrace, all strength and will, and my body reciprocated, to each movement, submissive as it had never been before.

And that first time already carried within it the kernel of what we would be all those other days, all those other nights. Your rage and your gentleness would alternate, but rage at what? That's what I'd ask myself, rage toward me? How could you be angry at me if you were there with me, and slept beside me, and embraced me. And how could I, right from the start, catch sight of that rage, feel it? But I did.

There were so many signs. The following day I woke up with my body in pain, bruises from my neck running in long shapes down my back, my legs, bruised, black and blue, purple, and I stood looking at myself in the mirror for some time, unable to remember, imagining that somehow, without noticing, I must have knocked into the side of the armchair, the corner of the bed, some accident. But may I make a confession? I confess that the following day, when you left, I would look at myself in the mirror and think I was beautiful, think I'd never been so beautiful, my face unrecognizable. My body so fragile and so lovely like that, an extreme loveliness, a unique loveliness. There was perfection in that fragility, the marks that accentuated it. And I confess that even the marks, even the pain was something I kept, the way one might keep a photo, a gift, a telephone number on a napkin. It was confirmation that you really had been there, you really had been there with me all night. Even if you left, even if you never wanted me again, never came back. I'd look at myself in the mirror and caress myself, and I saw in those patterns, in those marks, a symbol, a sign, something of yours that was so very intimate, and which I was the one to carry now.

A.

IV

Fabiane arrived at the restaurant half an hour late in a summer dress, light and low-cut. Her lateness was deliberate, of course. She came in apologizing, the traffic, she smiled, always the traffic. He tried not to show his annoyance, he smiled, lied that he'd also been late, yes, right, the traffic had been awful. They went on talking about the traffic for a few minutes, the waiter approached, they ordered something to drink. A glass of champagne for her, a beer for him.

Fabiane was the kind of woman who drank champagne in restaurants, and wherever she went, just like his ex-wife. He watched her for a few moments, noticing for the first time that, yes, the two women were very much alike, the

75

champagne, their way of dressing, even the way they were constantly arranging a lock of hair behind an ear. Even their demands, since nothing was enough, not ever. Octopus women, vampire women, wrapping around him, draining him of everything he had and then calling him selfish. That's how it always was. From the very look in their eyes, eyes that were carefully made up so as to look natural, ready to complain about everything, because nothing would do, the attention, the love, the affection, and the more he gave, the more dissatisfied they showed themselves to be, that constant air of reproach. He felt guilty, even if he didn't want to; perhaps he was sure that he could and should do much more. As though there were much more to do. Sometimes he felt insecure with them, other times, irritated like now. He wanted a woman who, rather than demanding, was inclined to give something in return. Not a princess looking down at him from her throne, but a real woman, a woman in love, attainable, capable of getting close and staying there, without fear, without expectations and without that protective distance. Just things the way they were. A woman ready even to lose and be lost for him. A woman ready to forgive. But perhaps this was no more than romanticism, he thought, self-centered romanticism, perhaps the product of some crisis he'd managed to glimpse but couldn't yet make out completely, a dejection, a discouragement, a discomfort that had begun with the birth of his daughter, gained in strength in recent years and now seemed ready to settle in for good. Pure romanticism, but why not, he thought, didn't he also have the right to want, to demand?

Fabiane sipped at her glass of champagne like his ex-wife, and he went on with his comparisons. Like his ex-wife, she was always careful, her movements finely calculated, impeccable; why not just drink, fearlessly, like a woman who drank vodka, tequila, who downed her drink in one gulp with a smile? But no, Fabiane was completely planned; she was like a mannequin in a shop window, as though at any moment someone might appear and surprise her and she would need to be ready. But the truth was, nobody would ever surprise her. Fabiane would never surprise anyone. He was furious.

Perhaps noticing his irritation, she said:

"Marcos?"

"What?"

"So, it looks like you're not that interested in what I'm telling you."

"Of course I am, I was just thinking about something else."

"In other words, you weren't paying attention."

"Of course I was, Fabiane, I got distracted for a second and thought about something else, that was all, it happens to everyone."

"What did you think about?"

"Whatever, I've forgotten, nothing important."

Fabiane didn't believe his explanation. She sipped a little more of her champagne. To change the subject, he suggested:

"So how about we order?"

"Why, are you in a hurry to leave?"

"No, Fabiane, I'm hungry, I'd like to order, that's all."

She glared at him, angry. Something between them wasn't working that night. But perhaps it had never worked, and it was only at that moment that he'd noticed. Since they'd first met (at the time he was still married), Fabiane had expected something more. After the separation, the demands started; since there was no longer anything to stop him, he had to make up his mind. Make up his mind about what, he'd asked, to be with her, she'd answered, to be with her properly. He'd argued with her: So up till now it's all been a lie then, I suppose, she'd laughed. After the separation there was Fabiane, it's true, but there was also solitude and other possibilities. A few girls he was friendly with, not very close, but pleasant, or perhaps pleasant for that reason. Girls who popped up from time to time and whose main function was ensuring that nobody should be allowed to take up too much space, especially not Fabiane. Even though time passes, we keep making the same mistakes, he thought. But he was not born for those girls, pleasant and distant, nor was he born for Fabiane.

"If I'd known how cranky you were going to be I'd have stayed home."

He pretended not to have heard the comment, finished drinking his beer and said:

"I watched a really interesting movie yesterday."

"Don't change the subject, Marcos, you always do that when you're not interested, you just change the subject, I think it's cowardly of you."

"Cowardly?"

"That's right, cowardly."

He paused slightly, trying to control himself, but eventually said:

"I do think, Fabiane, that you should think twice before just saying the first idiotic thing that comes into your head."

She didn't reply, she stood up, took her handbag. He thought she was going to leave, but no, she headed for the restroom. He stayed, toying with the empty glass, the cutlery, the napkin. He wasn't usually so harsh, actually, he'd never spoken to her like that, not even when they'd argued.

He had lost control and he didn't know why, he just felt such irritation, as though everything she said were an insult. But nothing about her had changed. He was the one who wasn't doing well. He shouldn't have bothered, he should have invented another excuse. Maybe something had changed, he dared to imagine, just like that, after reading the latest letter this morning.

But it was no use now, he would apologize, try to salvage something from the night. It troubled him that he was so bothered by those letters, which weren't even for him; he'd spent the whole day thinking about them, about the real addressee, the previous tenant. He'd talk to the doorman as soon as he got home, he'd ask for his forwarding address, telephone number, he'd even go to this guy's new place, deliver the letters, be rid of them at once. He didn't want to think any more about it now, even though he was thinking about it all the time, barely realizing it. He felt as though there were something subtly worming its way into him. But perhaps there was no subtlety about it at all.

Maybe ten minutes went by, then twenty, Fabiane hadn't returned, he noticed with surprise, so immersed was he in his thoughts. Perhaps she'd left, gone out the back door. He thought about going after her. But she ended up coming back from the bathroom with her eyes red, hair tucked behind her ear. She was a very beautiful woman, he thought

rather sadly, not sad for her, but for himself, for his impos-
sibilities, his inability to accept the way she was, accept her
company, simply to like her. She sat down without looking
at him. He put his hand on hers. He attempted a conciliatory tone.

"I'm sorry, I shouldn't have said that."

"No, fine, forget it." She was avoiding his gaze.

"I'm not doing great today."

"Has something happened?"

"No, nothing in particular, work stress, the usual."

She gave a little smile now. With the same speed at which
she became enraged, Fabiane was also quickly appeased,
he thought almost affectionately. Immediately the waiter
appeared with their meals. They ate their dinner. Both of
them pretending nothing had happened. They talked
about the things they usually talked about. He talked about
work, about the weekend, about his daughter, she complained about her mother, her sister, her family, she also
complained about being alone and about work. He ate a
lasagna, she had shellfish au gratin. He asked for another
beer, she asked for white wine. He tried to prevent his feelings of irritation from returning, from becoming so obvious again. She pretended not to notice.

When the dinner and conversation were approaching
their final moments, the check paid, one last sip before

leaving, the question came that he had been expecting, not quite so suddenly, but he had been expecting it.

"So what now?"

"What now, what?"

"Aren't you going to invite me around for a drink at your place?"

It was an invitation, no, it was a demand, he thought for a few moments. And she hadn't even waited till they'd gotten to the car. The easiest thing would be to say yes, to take her to his room, to his bed, but at that moment the easiest thing seemed much more difficult to him. A refusal wouldn't make things any better, but on the other hand he didn't want things to get any better. He thought about that morning. He didn't want it. All the same, it would never be easy to say no to a beautiful woman, and yet, at the same time, there was always a certain narcissistic pleasure to be had in saying no to a beautiful woman. He ought to say no more often. As an act of revenge.

"That's not going to work out today, Fabiane."

He inhaled deeply, a pause for breath, tried to arrange things in such a way that they didn't seem too important.

"I've got to be up early tomorrow, a meeting," he said, playing with his napkin.

A meeting was a fairly well-worn excuse, he could have thought of something better, more convincing, but the

truth was he really did have a meeting the following morning. Sometimes it was best not to tell the truth. Now it was
too late; he'd already said it.

"A meeting . . ." Fabiane looked at him in disbelief.

"Right, a meeting. And also, I'm really very tired, don't
take it the wrong way."

His own voice didn't ring true to him—"Don't take it the
wrong way, Fabiane"—he never talked like that. She seemed
to notice this, she probably felt rejected, repelled, all the
same she decided to pretend that it hadn't affected her.

"No, of course I won't take it the wrong way. It's for the
best, I've got to be up early tomorrow, too."

She seemed to be trying to think fast while she talked,
maybe trying to come up with the best response, a few
words that would rescue her from that discomfort as
quickly as possible, that would restore her poise, her ele-
gance, the manner she had of being the kind of person who
drank champagne. He offered:

"I'll call you later, we can arrange to meet up on the
weekend. What do you think?"

"Sure, let's arrange that."

He knew it was a lie, he wouldn't call, of course. She
knew it, too.

The night was over before ten, at least it was with Fabiane. He left her at home, saying goodbye to her in the car

outside her building. He gave her a quick kiss, trying to strip the moment of any dramatic coloring. She went inside without looking back. He pressed down on the accelerator carefully, as though afraid of being surprised, or worried that any noise might alert her, make her turn suddenly and come back toward him, knock on the window, her lips moving without his being able to hear her. But she didn't turn around. And he drove home thinking perhaps he had been unfair.

The truth was, he'd arrived at the restaurant already expecting not to enjoy it, whatever she said, not wanting it, so that events would take their course. And Fabiane, who knew nothing of the last few days, had no way of defending herself. He was probably being unfair. Now, sitting on the sofa in his apartment, he thought it was better this way, imagining that that had been their last meeting, but perhaps it wasn't, perhaps there was still room for others, but in any case, he would not be seeking her out again.

My darling,

It would be easier if it was only about the violence, the blood, the marks on my body after I saw you. And then I could love you or hate you deeply. But no. There were other nuances, other moments, sometimes there was a gentleness and I'd think, Where did this submissive manner of yours come from, this defenselessness, where could it have come from, all of a sudden.

There was something in you, some gentleness that moved me, as if you were also suffering the whole time. I would look at you in surprise and wonder. Why were you suffering? Those precious moments, after all the violence, all the hatred, that gentleness when you would lay your head in my lap and suffer, and I'd be there, scared of making any false move, any sound, any gesture that might snuff out that moment, that forgiveness, that silence uniting us. I would stroke your face very gently, the tips of my fingers over your brow, your temples, your eyes, the soft tips of my fingers on your long closed eyelashes, and I'd think, God, how beautiful your face was. Sometimes you'd fall asleep, your head still there in my lap—you always fell asleep quickly—and I'd be there beside you, my insomnia keeping me company, my vigil. Your face isn't a child's face in the way a man's face is when he's asleep, I've told you this before; a man when he's asleep is a man disarmed, a boy-man, but not you, in your face that uneasiness lingered, that distress. I've always been alarmed that someone can suffer in their sleep when everything is supposed to be so calm, as though that deepest suffering finally showed itself during your sleep, I used to think with your head in my lap for hours at night until dawn. I kept watch over your sleep, your nightmares, like a child, I was filled with that warmth, with that love, just thinking, I, who would give you anything; I, who could do anything, could carry you in my body and give birth to you and cradle you in my lap and feed you, and whisper an old song, something to soothe you, the tips of my fingers, still damp from my tears or from some other desire of my own. A love that was so great, do you understand?

That's right, there were other small moments and details, too. There always are. The secrets hidden in those cracks of the outward appearance, in the flaws of this character we've invented. And the following day, in the mirror, besides the marks and the pains, there was that gentleness, that gentleness inscribed there, and something incredibly beautiful, something that fascinated me, and that changed everything, it changed everything, do you understand?

But maybe you won't understand, or maybe you'll think I'm just repeating the same old things, something I've been saying for a long time. It's possible. And now I'm thinking, I wonder whether I really am saying what I'm saying? Maybe I'm being naive, maybe I think I am exposing myself, naked, fragile, talking to you about affection and gentleness, when in reality I'm destroying you, gladly, willingly. Maybe I'm being naive, maybe I think I am reconquering you—could I be reconquering you? When in reality what I'm doing is preparing something that will gradually move us further apart, something that will divide us definitively and move us further apart. Or, even worse, what guarantee do I have that what I say to you, what I'm making such a great effort to say to you, doesn't include other whims, other impulses, snaking their way in? The meanest, vilest things, without my wanting them to, without my knowing, get away from me; there's always something that gets away and betrays me. How to control the worst in me? Is it me, naive, destroying you, gladly, willingly, imagining that this is a kind of love?

And how am I to know, after all? How to know whether you've made it this far, this letter in your hands, if you had the courage, yes, because you'd need courage, you'd need courage to bear all this waiting and receive all this love, even if it's only a deception. And all these words that are always something else, how is it possible to know?

Writing is full of misunderstandings, just like speech. Not like a look, which is always revealing—there's nothing more revealing than a look, a distant look in the midst of such a great love, a wicked look during a declaration of innocence, or a clingy look when the body goes away. Could there be a way of saying things without the meaning getting away from us, is there any way of controlling our words? I could, for example, write a footnote to each line in this letter, an explanation for each line, telling you the source, where all this has come from—the pain, the doubt, your gentleness—a note telling you that where it says "table," it was really a room, and where it said "street," it was really a bed, not just any bed, but my bed and sheets, remember? I wonder whether your sheets and mine would be the same? And just to reassure myself, I'd send another note, for that day, that night, the last night, remember? And still the doubt remains, are our recollections of those days the same? And even, was it you, was it really you? Memory tends to deceive, memory and time and the desire for things to be the way we think they were, was it you, that day, that night, those sheets? The footnote at the bottom of the page would explain it all to you once again: where it says "hate," it was love, such a great love. And, if possible, I'd add some text to explain not only the words, but also to guide your reading. There, where there are simple, banal words, you would read instead something very beautiful, something unexpected, to make you come back, to make you love me and come back. Or even if you don't love me, let this reading be a kind of love, too. And we are left with this hope.

I say these things because I'm constantly alarmed at this impossibility between us. There was between us, always has been, a whole chain of falsely drawn conclusions, of misunderstandings.

At times there was some everyday reason for these misunderstandings. The two of us walking on the street, chatting, the street full of couples chatting about things that were obvious, everyday, and suddenly one of us would use a poorly chosen word—it was something I said, or didn't say, how was I to know—and suddenly nothing was as it had been, and your hand that had previously caressed my arm, your arm that had wrapped gently around me, the two of us chatting, your hand, your hand now squeezed me hard, your fingers digging into my arm, the skin losing its color, like that day at the rental place, remember? But many other days, too, we were someplace or other and it didn't even need to be your fingers squeezing my arm, it could be anything, the palm of your hand on my face, the sound and burning heat of the palm of your hand on my face, visible for a long time afterward, as though at every moment the gesture was being renewed, and was being renewed now, now, at this moment as I write to you, I bring my fingers to my cheek trying to feel it again, that pain, that burning and throbbing, the skin turned red. Where can it have come from, that hatred of yours? And then where did all that gentleness come from? And why is it that these movements, disparate as they are, merge together, at every moment, in me, in you? I think about that even now.

One day, it was maybe two, three weeks after our first meeting, our first look, I remember, I think it was during dinner, just any old day, right at the beginning, remember? I'd been spending the afternoon cooking and you arrived somehow strange, threw your backpack onto the sofa and said nothing, that silence of yours. I kept talking to calm you down, to calm myself down, talking about the food, about the ingredients, the supermarket, perhaps just to lessen my anxiety and—why not—my fear, I kept talking, and I asked you questions, remember? I couldn't stop doing that, asking questions, not because I expected an answer but like a child, my hand seeking out yours, have I told you that already? At first you replied in monosyllables, later not even that, but I kept talking, my hand seeking out yours, insisting. I set the table, put the food on the table, as you sat silent in front of the television, I told you dinner was ready, and you sat there, unmoving in front of the television, remember? When you sat down at the table at last, the television was still on so I got up, turned it off, said something like: I don't like having dinner with the TV on, something like that. You said nothing, there was only your look and the distance it imposed. I could barely get the food down my throat for the feeling that I'd said something wrong again, something awful. You were serious as you ate, silent, as if you hated me, or as if you were suffering. Where could it have come from, all that suffering? I asked you something again about the food, the ingredients, the supermarket, I don't remember exactly, do you? But I know there was a last question, and suddenly your hand pushed the plate off the table, the noise of the plate and the food on the plate falling off the table, the noise of the plate, and the food on the floor next to the table, and you, I remember your words exactly, you raised your voice and said, in that tone that always used to paralyze me: Will you shut your fucking mouth. Will you shut your fucking mouth. Those words look so strange to me written here, like another language. And I thought that was an unbearable violence. Those words, the whole gesture that went with them, the plate and the food spread across the floor.

I stayed there unmoving, tears streaming down my face, how many times did I have tears streaming down my face; I always repeat myself. And I stayed where I was, while you went back to sitting in front of the television; how much time went by while you were in front of the television and I sat there, looking at my plate that was still on the table, tears streaming down my face? And that was a violence, I thought and kept thinking, a violence.

Until I got to my feet at last and began to clean up what was left of that day, of that dinner. The plate and the food spread across the floor, and everything that was left over from that gesture of yours and those words of yours, "your fucking mouth," wasn't that it? How much time went by? I don't know, maybe an hour, maybe a year, I don't know. All I know is that when I finished cleaning up, your gesture, your words, you were still there in front of the television, and I was sitting in a chair in a corner of the living room, my legs tightly closed together, hands on my knees, as though I were being punished, as though I'd done something terrible. I sat there for hours on that chair; time seemed to have stagnated. I was alarmed to see you like that, it was the first time I'd seen you that way, and I had this desire to get up, to leave or, more logically, to send you away, it was my house, my sofa, my television, how was it possible? Still I sat on that chair, legs together.

Until you, still sitting on the sofa, looked at me with contempt and said: Come on, stop crying, come sit here.

You said it like someone granting a concession, like someone finally granting forgiveness, Come sit here, as though I were the guilty one. I got up, almost happy, have I told you that already? At that moment I was almost happy, when I got up off the chair, it surprised me, how was it possible? I walked very slowly toward you, my back aching, my whole body aching from those words of yours, from that gesture, my body suddenly felt heavy, and I was dragging it, while you were sitting there, Come here, you were saying, it was a rescue, a command.

I approached slowly, and when I made as if to sit down next to you, at that same moment you pulled my arm, hard, fitting me into your lap, surprising me. It was such a great love, what I felt for you, such a great love. I'd been through hell, and now you were holding out a hand to me and all was well again. And it was a desperate kind of happiness, could there be any such thing, a desperate happiness? All was well again and I hugged you and kissed you longingly, furiously, I tore off your clothes and hurt my fingers tearing off your clothes, the expectation of your naked body, your skin, like never before, and finally, seeing you naked, your naked body, How could it be so beautiful, your naked body, I thought, how was it possible, that beauty, that arrogance? I shed my own clothes, hardly giving myself enough time, and lifted up my skirt and opened my legs and sat on your lap, sat slowly on your lap, my legs open, my gaze clinging to yours, my body a perfect fit as it descended. I felt something like a fall, a weakening, the meeting of our nakedness, the precision of your skin on the most delicate outlines of my skin, and the brushing of my breasts against your chest, against your mouth. I embraced you deeply and kissed you, more and more, my tongue caressing yours. I arched and unarched my body, whispering promises and incoherent words in your ear, saying the most obscene words in your ear and scratching you, gripping and biting and squeezing you, feeling the sweat running down my face, and my body arched and unarched and seemed all liquid, all flow, all blood. And I was nothing but a slow, endless moaning. And at each moment I thought, How was it possible? How could such things be possible, this abyss, this happiness?

A.

V

He thought about the difficulty he'd had in focusing for the minutes in the car that morning, perhaps longer, when he was shut away in the car, in the garage, the difficulty he'd had in starting the day, after the hours dragged past as he asked about something at a meeting at work, in English, an incredibly important meeting, in a suit, in a tie, first thing in the morning. He'd acted like an idiot, he knew, his thoughts distant and fragmented, his colleagues throwing him questioning looks: So what was that about? someone had asked him discreetly as they left. Nothing, he replied, escaping as quickly as he could, leaving no time for any more questions.

So what did he mean by his behavior, then? That was

what everyone was wondering, that was what he was wondering himself—was he planning to get fired? Other people would have lost their jobs for much less, but he had all that efficiency, that punctuality, that responsibility. He had been on edge for several days now. And he also felt a certain inexplicable irritation. A kind of bad mood. He went to the restroom, took off his tie, loosened his collar, washed his face, an attempt to wake up once and for all.

On the way to his office, he registered the intern who always walked past him unnoticed, but today he stopped by her desk. He looked at her closely. Daniela seemed just out of adolescence, her face elastic and rounded, smiling at anyone who passed. He came a little closer, but her attention was on her computer.

"Daniela, what do you think about receiving letters?"

She looked up, intrigued.

"Letters?"

"Yeah, letters, I don't mean e-mails, faxes, text messages. I'm talking about letters on paper, the kind you send in the mail."

She still didn't react. He insisted:

"Have you ever received a personal letter?"

"I don't remember, maybe, why?"

"And what did you think?"

"About what? About the letter?"

"No, not about the letter itself, about the fact of receiving it."

"I don't know, I don't remember, if I got one it was a long time ago, maybe when I was a kid."

"Right, but if you got a letter now? If you arrived home tonight and when you went to look in your mailbox you found a letter. With your name on it, your address, a stamp, a postmark, or without a postmark, that doesn't matter."

"I don't know. It would depend on the letter, what it said."

"A love letter, say."

"A love letter, oh, I'd think that was romantic."

"Would you fall in love?"

"I don't know, but I imagine that if it's a love letter, I would be in love already, wouldn't I?"

"Not necessarily, Daniela, let's say it was a love letter from someone you knew only superficially, would you fall in love?"

"I don't know, it would depend on the person, on what the letter said . . . oh, I don't know, so many things."

"But you'd think it was romantic."

"Yes."

"Would you think it was beautiful?"

"Yeah, I guess."

"And the person, what would you think of them?"

"I don't know, it would depend on the person."

"Would you find them interesting?"

"Yes, maybe."

"And would you think they were different from other people?"

"Yes, definitely."

"Thank you, Daniela, that was all I wanted to know."

The intern followed him with her gaze until he entered his office. She flicked her hair back several times, cracked her knuckles several times. She opened her drawer, took out a notepad, only to put it straight back in again. She closed the drawer and tried to focus back on her computer.

In his office, he was working on a report that he should have been finishing, he made a few phone calls, replied to e-mails, tidied some of the mess on his desk and went out for lunch. He got a roasted chicken from the bakery. It had been years since he'd eaten a roasted chicken. He sat on one of the stools at the counter. Rice, beans, and French fries on the side. He thought he could eat that forever, without any trouble at all. He was a man of simple tastes, none of this luxury restaurant business, women's luxuries, like his ex-wife, Fabiane and every woman he knew, the women who would never be satisfied with a chicken from the bakery, to whom a bakery chicken would even be an insult, a mark of disrespect. Even Daniela, the intern who couldn't say how she'd feel if she received a letter, would have looked at his plate scornfully. Maybe even Manuela, his three-year-old daughter.

The world of women is a closed-off world, he thought, a world apart. And he was surrounded by women on all sides; unlike certain men who felt more at ease with them, he didn't, and it bothered him, that sense that nothing he was or did would be enough. The truth was, women scared him, and at the same time, led him to experience feelings that were confusing and contradictory.

Instead of going back to work after lunch, he took his car and drove around and around the city, giving no thought to whether or not he should be doing this, just the idea that he needed to get far away, to leave, without really leaving. He called his assistant and notified her that something unexpected had come up, that he'd be back later. He was in the car now, closed off, hermetic, safe in the city. After a while, he parked close to a little square, got out of the car, considered sitting on a bench or playing checkers with the retirees, waiting there for the day to go by. He considered returning home, or even going back to the office. But he ended up going into a snack bar, ordering a random soda; the guy behind the counter looked at him with a smile. He was opposite a post office, he noticed with some surprise. He leaned on the snack bar counter and stayed there, just watching the people going in and out of the post office. He was seeing a lot of retirees, he thought, only retirees write letters, have time to go to the post office, retirees, students, maybe someone looking for work, for an internship. He was imagining a young woman, attractive, well dressed—is that what she'd be like? Like all women. He was imagining his ex-wife. For some reason whenever he imagined a woman it was always the same woman, but not this time, she was somebody different this time, she wasn't Fabiane, or his ex, or any of the girls he kept at a prudent distance; he realized how hard it was to imagine a different somebody. Maybe the woman from the movie he'd seen the other day, just one of the five he'd rented, in a red dress, a folder under her arm, the noise of her heels on the little sidewalk paving stones, a woman who fixes her hair before walking into the post office.

The post office is a small one, and from where he's sitting in the snack bar, it's possible to see the people standing in line, it would be possible to see a woman who is well dressed but different from the others, inside her folder a blue envelope, the careful rounded hand, her long black hair tied at the nape of her neck; she looks from side to side, perhaps knowing she's being watched, perhaps looking for somebody, a certain ambiguity about her, she looks one way as though looking the other, her slim fingers holding the envelope—a whole scene that he has imagined. Watching from the snack bar, his soda untouched on the counter, he imagines that the woman would wear a tight skirt, a silk blouse and high-heeled sandals. She might be a secretary on her lunch break: the woman wears glasses with heavy black frames, she looks serious, unattainable, but her body has a certain voluptuousness that gives her away. She walks into the post office, waits in line. When she reaches the counter, she takes the blue envelope out of the folder, hands it to the clerk. The clerk remarks that the sender's name is missing. The woman is giving off a slight sense of concern, but only to anybody looking very closely. Her reply to the clerk is confident:

"No, it's right the way it is."

The clerk doesn't seem very convinced. She's young and uncertain, she thinks maybe it's illegal to send a letter without a named sender, she's uncertain.

"I think that's not allowed, not having a sender."

"What do you mean, 'not allowed'? Since when?"

"It is not permitted," replies the clerk, somewhat intimidated by the woman's self-assurance.

"Of course it is. I come here every day. Call your superior over, I'd like to speak to him."

The woman looks even more beautiful at this moment,

he thinks. And he thinks that the woman has started going back to resembling his ex-wife, or Fabiane. That arrogant, almost insolent manner, the energy that used to intimidate him. When all he wanted was a certain something in their eyes, someone who has nothing to lose, someone who has lost her fear. That's what they're like, people who have lost their fear, sharp and sweet at the same time. Maybe that was what attracted him in those letters, this woman who was sharp and sweet. The presence he tried to imagine, without success. The clerk might have thought or felt something similar; she told herself it was best not to seek out trouble on her very first week at work. She thought it best to give in.

"All right, that won't be necessary." The clerk took the letter and franked it, a mark that was rather faded but on which it was possible to see the location of the post office.

The woman said nothing, she didn't thank the clerk, didn't complain. She just opened her bag, took out a small leather purse and paid the amount due. Then she left the post office, he imagined, walking down the street in the haughty manner of someone who is fearless. Then he tried not to think about her anymore, about what might have been an explanation, even if he ruined it at every moment; he went back to thinking about his ex-wife and Fabiane. His ex-wife and Fabiane, as though they were one and the same person, so alike, deep down, the same braveries and cowardices. Maybe we always choose the same person, he thought, looking at the glass of soda.

He thought Manuela was just like his ex-wife, who was just like Fabiane, who was just like all the possible women in his imagination, and Manuela was only three years old. At fifteen she would be called Manu for good, she would have an unacceptable boyfriend and she'd constantly be hooking her red hair behind her ear. At fifteen she would display evident indifference toward him. And he would see her all ready to go out, would ask, Manuela, where are you going? and she'd reply, a note of boredom in her voice, You know, out, her eyes always looking off somewhere, and chewing gum. He'd ask with whom, she'd say, Some friends; he'd insist, Which friends? and she would say, with a mixture of boredom and impatience, You know, some friends of mine, her eyes always looking off somewhere, and chewing gum, the noise of the gum being chewed bothering him more and more; he'd tell her to throw the gum away, she'd throw it on the floor, and he'd want to whack her and would regret never having given her a whack. But at fifteen he would already have given up. And what was more, she was only a three-year-old girl. He preferred not to think about Manuela.

He felt uneasy. He paid for the soda, for the parking

spot, got back into the car. He spent the rest of the afternoon driving around the city with no fixed route, just this,
the closed-off car and the city out there. He thought he
would arrive home, but kept putting it off and at the same
time he was anxious to get home, because he'd been feeling
that anxiety for days, a difficulty in focusing.

Even at work he had been making plans, that as soon as
he got home he'd talk to the doorman, he'd get the address
of the former tenant and at last he'd return the letters, he'd
say he opened them just in case, all of them, trying to find
his name, a new address, or he'd just say he had opened
them and that was that, not explaining too much. He'd arrive home, talk to the doorman and then, feeling calmer,
free, revived, he'd call Fabiane, apologize, invite her for dinner, to go for a drive, whatever she wanted. He would say
that he had been confused, some trouble at the office, but
that he wasn't confused anymore. Anxiety, he thought,
would get him to call Fabiane. Even while knowing that, no,
he would arrive home without speaking to anyone, he'd
open the door, deposit the correspondence on the table and
turn on the TV; he would put a movie in the DVD player
and let his thoughts be extinguished before they even took
shape.

My darling,

I'd promised myself I wouldn't talk about that day anymore, about the rental place, the movie, the actor so like you, the character. I'd promised. You complain I'm always repeating myself, and with good reason. Why keep going back to the same subjects, to the same things that have been laid bare, pored over so many times, the rental place, the actor, the movie, that day.

You must be wondering, with good reason. And you must be thinking I never keep my promises. But it's not true. In my defense I can argue that the rental place today is never the same as yesterday's, that between one and the other, time goes by. Our time, ours, do you understand? The time that gets itself in between the words and all your turns and returns. Between this letter and the first there is a whole unraveling of facts and consequences and memories, between this and the first reading, a whole unfolding, filling up, distorting what I so fervently wanted to say since the beginning, remember? Because, however much I want to repeat myself, again and again, what I have said to you is never what I say to you now.

And if, at that first moment when you sat in your living room, on the sofa, the chair, in an armchair, with the first letter in your hands, if at that moment you felt rage or curiosity or any other feeling, now, the same words, the chair, the armchair, now, even if we try to reproduce every detail, like in the theater, in a play, you forever receiving the first letter, me forever repeating the same words, the result would be different each time, even if it's once again the old rage or curiosity or some other feeling. Like in the theater. Or in a movie or a book to which you return from time to time like someone returning to a place they do not know. And you're surprised to find that what is unknown is not the place, the furniture and shadows and colors, all of it so familiar, what's unknown is you, however hard you try and however often you keep reciting the old words and old verses by heart. However great the effort and the intention and the will, there is always something to surprise and alarm you.

But perhaps you think everything I'm telling you now I'm only saying in order to justify myself, to justify this insistence, this monotony of mine. Perhaps that's what you think, you think me capable of constructing the most varied plots, the most complex theories, even a reader for these letters, isn't that it? A character to receive these letters in your place. Someone to read for you and guide you and say to you, Yes, there's something very beautiful, isn't there? There's nothing I could not do just to convince you to maybe, who knows, go back to the very beginning. All this, then, just to be able to go back now, once again, to the precise moment of beginning. The two of us walking, the rental place, the movie, that actor or character so like you. Your fingers on my arm. Except that the beginning is never the same.

That day, after the rental place, we arrived home in silence, both of us. I put my fingers to my arm, where yours had been earlier, as though protecting myself, grieving for myself. I thought something would happen. I always thought something would happen. Often I would kid myself and a day would go by with no harm done, and then on other days, the most astonishing things would happen.

We arrived home and I opened the front door to the house, my door, my house. You went in, threw the bag of bread onto the table, sat down on the sofa, opened the newspaper and started reading. I just stood there for a few moments, considering saying something, anything, something that would drive us apart, something that would unite us. But there was nothing to say. I hung my bag on the chair and went into the kitchen to make the coffee.

The coffee grinder was the first and only gift you gave me. That's just how you were when it came to coffee, you were crazy about it. A whole series of minutely detailed rules for preparing it. A particular kind of bean, roasted in some certain way or other, kept in the fridge in a sealed container. You didn't trust me and you came over yourself to check the sealed container. You showed up one day with that coffee grinder package, really it wasn't even a present for me, but I wanted it to be and acted as though it was. You showed up saying, I've brought you a present, but it wasn't, I thought, you put the package down on the table and turned on the TV. I didn't move, just looked at the package, and you were looking for some program or other on the TV. Aren't you going to open it, you asked as you channel surfed. And because I really wanted it to be a present, I approached the package and opened it.

The paper was ordinary wrapping paper, I remember, then I finally opened it and out came the coffee grinder. It's imported, you said. It was automatic, I read on the box. "Automatic coffee-grinding machine," or something like that, in Italian. I thanked you and just sat there, sitting, really wanting it to be a gift. Later you explained to me how it worked, So easy, just press a button, you said, and I agreed, and we set the machine up just below the microwave. Coffee should always be ground at the time you want to make it, you said. But why, I asked, what difference does it make, and my question was the trigger you needed to give me an explanation of all the subtleties between normal coffee powder and the freshly ground kind. But that wasn't all, there was also the water and the temperature of the water and the pressure and the milk, absolutely no milk under any circumstances, you said, nobody who really knows their coffee would ruin it by adding milk, much less sugar. And to please you, I followed every one of your whims, the cup of perfect bitter coffee on the table. I did so many things just to please you, I think now, just to please you.

I made the coffee, put the just-bought bread on top of the fridge. I wasn't hungry and you were never hungry; Only the coffee, you'd say. I put the cup down on the little side table next to you as you sat reading your newspaper. I said: Here's the coffee. Said it as though it was necessary to make an announcement. You said nothing, I stood there, right in front of you, waiting for an answer. Anything. You said nothing.

I sat down far away, at the dining table, stayed there, examining the little scratches in the wood that I hadn't noticed before. I tried to think about the rental place, to understand what had just happened to us, but I couldn't do it, my thoughts got themselves all tangled, in the scratches in the wood, in the cup of coffee.

Could it be that I realized, as I ask myself now, could it be that I realized something had changed, do we really realize when things happen, right at the moment when things happen? Or do we maybe only realize later? Hours, days, years later, when we think about these moments, when we feel them, when we recount them. Or are they happening perpetually in another moment? An unreachable moment. Because they are happening now, once again, as I write to you, and once again I feel the same distress, the same fear: you sitting there, just reading. You sitting there now, reading silently. Once again I feel the distress and the sense that something's happened, something unspeakable. Once again the coffee and the table and the movie and your hands. Will things really never stop happening?

You didn't say a word that afternoon. I even asked, as a way of reaching a hand out toward you, You want a glass of water? You want more coffee? But you didn't answer. You went on reading your newspaper, a whole heap of paper that was scattered across the furniture, across the living room, and when that was over and you were finished, you turned on the television, you changed channels every two minutes, then picked up a book, then a magazine, then watched the television again; time refused to pass, as you sat there, motionless.

And as it got dark, I came apart, something was dissolving away in me. At first, sitting at that table, still, as though hypnotized, watching the newspaper, the book, hearing the noise from the television, as though I wasn't there. Then the thoughts came and went, always the same images: the rental place, the movie, the actor or character who was so like you or wasn't, could that really be so important, a secret that got in between us, a betrayal, something appalling I'd hidden, was there something, was there something appalling I didn't know about but which was mine? From one moment to the next, somebody was losing their memory, the memory of a whole series of another person's treacheries, so different in reality, perhaps an actor, a character, and I think, maybe that's really what it's like, one day the movements that aren't mine, those same movements, the gap between them, something in which I recognize myself, at last I recognize myself, something mean and unpredictable, the greatest betrayals, as the world went on, still you sat there, a newspaper, a book, and still I sat there silently before you, the greatest betrayals.

At a certain point I couldn't bear it, I asked a question once again, searched for your hand. You didn't answer, I got to my feet, my mind made up. But my mind made up to do what? That's what I wondered. I got to my feet and went into the bedroom, maybe to force you to apologize to me, to follow me, but you were still, impassive.

In the bedroom your things were scattered about, I picked up your backpack, put it on the chair, or was that afterward? I don't know anymore. But I just remember your things scattered around, your backpack, your laptop on the table. I'd cleared everything off that table for you, and I would have rearranged the whole house for you, my house, I would have rearranged the whole house for your books, for your clothes, and I would have accepted your obsessions, the coffee, the sheets, the towel, anything you wanted, even myself, I would even have reinvented myself, anything to please you. But you didn't want that, your need, your distance, that apartment of yours, where you sit now, perhaps with a cup of coffee, this letter in your hands. Why? Maybe because you knew that, in spite of everything, in spite of all the effort, the coffee, the sheets, the towels, in spite of all the effort, there was something that revealed me and betrayed me.

I stayed in the bedroom a few hours, I no longer remember what I did. I tidied up your things, looked out the window, read, I no longer remember. No, that's a lie, I do remember. I walked around the room, paced from end to end, straightened a picture on the wall, looked at myself in the mirror. I thought myself so obvious, so normal, I, who so desired you to see me, to desire me. At that moment, what I most wanted was for you to desire me. I took off my dress. Naked, in just my underwear, I looked even more beautiful, I thought, my body slim and soft, extremely soft, remember? You used to tell me that, your fingers stroking my back, the palm of your hand on my back.

I approached the mirror, took the black pencil out of the makeup case and circled my eyes, my darkened eyes, bestowing a new depth on them, almond eyes, they could be a gypsy's eyes, they could be the most exotic eyes, these eyes of mine, with that new depth. But seeing myself in the mirror, I still found myself obvious, predictable, something missing, that appalling something, which could surprise you, and make you smile or suffer, wasn't that it? Even if it was no more than a detail, a touch, just something abstract.

I went over to the dresser and took from the jewelry box a pearl necklace, a thin necklace, triple-looped, which had belonged to my grandmother and which I'd never worn. Then I examined myself again, just in my underwear, black cotton, and now wearing the pearl necklace that shifted between my breasts and made me somehow ancient and fragile, or even more naked. Why was I doing this, some kind of need to be nostalgic, I thought, perhaps to seduce you, perhaps because I thought something appalling was being revealed. In the mirror, however, I was just a nearly naked woman who was wearing a pearl necklace, my skin soft under my fingers as I very gently stroked my neck, around my breasts, my waist, as though wanting to reassure myself that what I was seeing was me.

But what I was seeing was always something else, something very different, a stranger, somebody much farther away than you are there, sitting on the sofa in your living room. I wondered if you were still there. The unending newspaper for the whole day. Suddenly I felt concern, doubt, the fear that you'd gone. I looked out the window, it was beginning to get dark, I was looking at your backpack on the table and your things, to reassure myself that, no, you were still there, that nothing had changed, that nothing could change. But I was still concerned. I opened the closet, took out a black tank top, tight and plain, thin straps that insisted on slipping off my shoulders. I kept the pearl necklace on, put on those high-heeled sandals you liked, the ones that hurt, remember?

Then I went back into the living room. Dressed like that, the underwear, the tank top, the pearl necklace. The noise of the sandals on the wooden floor. You were still there, unmoving. I went to the kitchen, opened the fridge and stood there, the fridge door open, for how long? I took out a bottle of water, filled a glass, put the bottle in the fridge, closed the door. I left the glass of water on the kitchen table, went out to the balcony, took the laundry down off the line, folded it, put it in the clean-clothes basket. I went back into the kitchen, picked up the glass, threw the water into the sink, dried the glass, put it away in the cupboard. I took another glass, filled it nearly halfway with vodka, neat vodka, drank a little, thought it tasted disgusting, drank half of it, threw the rest into the sink. I went back into the living room. You were still there. The noise of the sandals. My pearl necklace. I took a chair, sat down in front of you. I was a woman with heavily made-up eyes and a pearl necklace that contrasted with the dark fabric of the tank top and panties. My hair loose. The straps of the top slipping off my shoulders, the material barely covering my breasts. My legs on display. You said nothing. It had been hours since you'd said anything, how was that possible? Where did you get that scorn from, that strength? Without once looking at me. I started to cry, finally, I started to cry. You said nothing. You said once that my crying didn't move you, I remember: Crying doesn't move me, you said. And I knew you were being serious, and I hated you deeply and thought about something that might move you, something so strong, so alarming, so disconcerting that it would move you, dismantle you, destroy you, something that would make you suffer. But you weren't suffering. Sitting there, never once looking at me. You never suffered. How was it possible to have that scorn, that strength?

Maybe now, reading this letter in your apartment with a glass of water, a cup of coffee, reading it now, perhaps you see that I'm contradicting myself, once again, I'm always contradicting myself. Maybe you still remember the other letters, only the other day, could it have been yesterday? Only the other day I said that you slept and that you cried and that you suffered, or something in you suffered, something unreachable in you suffered, was that it? And how is it possible for you to have changed so much from one letter to the next? Yes, how was it possible? I'm contradicting myself, you're right, I'm contradicting myself. But I think, now, perhaps it's precisely in this contradiction, in this space that opens up between what I claim and what I deny, between your suffering and your cruelty, between my suffering and my cruelty, between my body and yours, in precisely this incoherence—this is the only means of communication. Isn't this space, this gap, the only place we can possibly meet?

A.

VI

Hi, Marcos, it's Fabiane—you okay? . . . I wasn't going to call you, actually I'd promised myself I wouldn't call you . . . but I don't know, I guess I just got worried, are you okay? That day at the restaurant I thought you seemed strange, did something happen? And today I've been trying to call you all day, why aren't you answering your cell? Or don't you want to talk to me? If that's what it is, just tell me once and for all. I've called your phone several times throughout the day, and I keep getting your voice mail. I called you at work, they said you haven't been in today, is that true? I'm worried something might have happened . . . Anyway, look, I won't keep bothering you, but I really need to talk to you. Let's talk, we really got to talk. Call me, even if you get in late. I won't be able to sleep anyway, you can call anytime . . . and we'll arrange something. I think it's important we talk, it was weird that day, wasn't it? You were . . . I don't know, you were different. Did something happen? Anyway, call me, I'll be waiting . . . Really do call, though. Lots of love, bye."

He listened to the other messages: two from the office, wanting something, a friend canceling a beer that he'd forgotten about himself, a girl studying architecture he'd recently met at a party, the rental place attendant saying the movies were overdue, somebody who'd called but changed their mind and hung up without leaving a message. He heard each one without paying much attention, ending with his ex-wife complaining about something:

"Where have you been all day, Marcos? I've been trying to get through to you since early this morning. I called yesterday and you didn't answer. This is impossible, I called the office and nobody there knows anything, and apparently you've decided not to answer your cell. Do me a favor and call as soon as you can. Just to remind you, in case you're at all interested, next week is Manu's birthday, your daughter, Manu, in case you've forgotten. I'm going to have a little party for her at her school, I hope you'll deign to show up. Don't worry about a present, just leave that to me and I'll buy something, you can give me the money later. Call me."

He didn't call her, didn't call anybody. He put the package down on the table, the package he hadn't realized he'd been holding on to since he arrived. At the same moment he felt the relief of being freed of an unexpected burden, relief, and he was surprised. He went into the kitchen, opened the fridge, took out some cheese and what was left in the bag of bread, went into the living room, spread everything out on the table, opened a can of beer. His ex-wife would certainly have had a comment to make about the way he was eating, without a plate, without any silverware, he thought with a smile.

He turned on the TV, put the movie in the DVD player, the same images on the screen that had accompanied him every night that week. The man, the woman in his arms, it could have been any movie, he thought, it could be the same movie every time, that was exactly the point. This time he thought it better to keep the lights on. He sat down and started eating, paying little attention to what he was doing.

He had been out all day, back to the snack bar opposite the post office. The guy behind the counter had greeted him as though he'd known him for a while, as though he'd been expecting him. He'd arrived early this time. He hadn't even stopped in at the office; he'd called in first thing that morning with some excuse. He was worried as he hung up, not about the lie he'd told or about not going into work, but about what he had in mind—the snack bar, the post office— the truth was that he didn't really know what exactly he was doing.

He parked close by, and as he approached, his anxiety increased with the feeling that he'd arranged to meet someone, to meet someone he hadn't seen for years, or to meet a stranger, one of those encounters that require you to wear a flower in your lapel or gaudy colors in order to identify yourself. There were countless ways of not recognizing someone, he thought, as he leaned against the snack bar counter. There were countless ways of meeting back up with someone. He ordered a coffee, paid for it in advance. Maybe he was considering a possible need to leave abruptly, to go someplace, perhaps to the post office right there across the street, with people walking by, cars stopped at the lights. Maybe there would be somebody in a hurry, a young woman, thin, with long black hair, a letter in her hands, the blue envelope, the rounded handwriting there was no way he could actually see but which he knew so well. He imagined being able to recognize her immediately. He would talk to her, he'd say something: that he'd received her letters, that he awaited them anxiously every day, that he had read them all several times, one by one, that there was something in them, in that surrender, in that intimacy, that got to him, even if he didn't understand it yet. He'd say there was something in him that was being transformed, or that had always been there. He'd say he understood her, that he, so different, so distant, a stranger, that he understood her. He would say this and much more, he imagined.

He stood there, his eyes alert, looking at each person who came out and each person who approached. He didn't even notice an old man beside him, dressed sloppily but not a vagrant; you could tell he was just an ordinary man, maybe a retiree, this man who had appeared without his noticing, who then said:

"This place is a dump, a dump . . ."

He started, he wasn't sure whether the old man was addressing him or talking to himself. He preferred not to answer. The old man went on, pointing his index finger in some unspecific direction:

"A dump, this place . . . Ever since the Portuguese fellow went. The staff now, they're a gang of layabouts, they do whatever they want, they do it on purpose, sure, they do it on purpose . . ."

And gesturing with his hand to make it quite clear that absolutely everything there was on purpose:

"Just look, a dump, just look . . ."

He remained silent while the old man went on:

"Worse every day, a dump . . ." And the word "dump" came out with drops of saliva that would have landed on him had he not instinctively taken a step back.

The old man shook his head to emphasize his observation. Dump. Then, looking at his cup:

"If I were you, I wouldn't even drink that," his finger practically in the cup, "garbage . . ."

The old man spat on the floor, in a gesture that seemed intended to underline what he was feeling. Garbage. He thought about what he might say, perhaps to agree. But at that moment somebody appeared, probably an employee of the snack bar, took the old man by the arm and led him outside, forcefully but not roughly. The old man didn't even protest; on the contrary, he allowed himself to be led, like a wound-up mechanical doll, he left on his own, dragging his flip-flops, shuffling along the pavement, his faint voice and complaints still audible. Garbage.

He remained there, in the snack bar; an employee with a forced smile apologized, assuring him that the old man was harmless—he comes in every day, practically a tourist attraction, with the few customers here just pretending nothing's happening. He agreed and looked uncertainly at his cup of coffee.

He thought about the old man for a few moments

longer, only to realize with some surprise that he'd taken his attention entirely off the post office, perhaps at a crucial moment. He was annoyed at having been so easily distracted. Who was to say he hadn't missed something important? And whatever we miss we miss forever, time never turns back, that's how these things are, he thought, somewhat discouraged. He spent the rest of the morning staring at the post office on the other side of the street, his coffee cold now, forgotten in the cup.

But perhaps it wasn't this post office? He took the letters out of his pocket, he examined the postmark on each blue envelope, some had a postmark, others didn't, the same notation repeated so many times. No, this was the one, the right post office, it had to be, and he put the letters back into his pocket. He'd make a terrible detective, he thought with a smile, his first of the day—what else did he have left if not the ability to laugh at himself, spending the whole day just sitting there like an idiot. It made no sense at all, he thought. He ordered another coffee, drank it quickly, paid and left.

As he walked toward his car, however, he changed his mind, made a little detour, walked past the front of the post office for one last look as the post office was closing, the last letters of the day. He stopped there a few moments longer and then kept going down the street, looking in the shop windows, just a quick glance at some of them, stopping in front of others, sometimes he moved to go in, but never did. After about half an hour, he finally went into the store he'd been looking for, the saleswoman approached, asked with a saleswoman's smile whether he wanted something, and he smiled back, but without taking much notice. Was he looking for something, she asked again; he said that yes, he was looking for a coffee machine.

"Coffee machine? A percolator?"

"No, it's a kind of machine."

"An espresso machine?"

"Yes, could be."

The saleswoman didn't stop smiling. She showed him several espresso machines, and he looked at them, trying to find in them some answer, some sign. Several minutes passed, the saleswoman gradually beginning to show traces of impatience.

"Were you looking for any particular model, sir?"

She'd called him "sir." At a certain moment that had started happening, saleswomen had started calling him "sir"; soon Manuela's friends would take to calling him "Uncle" Marcos, soon time would pass quickly.

"No, I'm just looking," he replied drily.

"The one you're looking at now, sir, that's the most modern model we have, it's only just come out, it's Italian."

"Ah . . . right."

"It can make up to twelve cups."

He smiled, continuing his examination of the other models.

"This one makes only six cups, but it's much more economical."

He didn't answer. After a few minutes, the saleswoman gave up; she was already walking away when he drew a blue envelope out of his pants pocket and said:

"Wait a moment."

The saleswoman turned around at once, perhaps surprised at his commanding tone. She made an effort to keep smiling as he took a bundle of crumpled papers out of the envelope, a letter, opened it, looking for something, perhaps some information about the machine.

"It's not a machine to make coffee, it's a machine to grind coffee."

"Oh, we don't have any grinders. But we should be getting one next week. Do you want to leave your number? I'll let you know as soon as it's here."

He shook his head, said nothing for a few moments, the saleswoman thinking he had given up, but then he put the letter and the envelope away in his pocket and pointed at the espresso machine, the six-cup one. In that case I'll take this one, he said, and she smiled. He paid quickly at the register, in cash, no, he didn't want it wrapped as a gift, no, he didn't want a warranty or anything explained, as quick as possible, the saleswoman watching him somewhere between suspicious and amused; he picked up the package and left the store without saying goodbye. She tried to say something after him—thank you, see you next time, come again, something like that—but he was already out the door.

He walked quickly to his car, almost ran, the package heavy in his hands. He paid for the parking, and left that place, that place where nothing happened, he thought disappointedly, that static part of the city, a story he'd made up, and which made no sense at all.

In the car he put the package down on the back seat, covered it up with the jacket he'd brought with him but hadn't worn, closed the door unnecessarily hard. Just turning on the air-conditioning, he started to feel better already. The cold air on his face, the windows closed, driving unhurriedly down the city streets, a set route, only the landscape changing. And he went back to thinking about the next day, about what he'd do, about what there was still to be done, as though he were sketching out a plan.

My darling,

Okay, so I'm sure I've done something wrong, something terrible, something unspeakable. Like a killer who has erased the moment of the crime from her memory, and is now just harmonious, gentle, all in balance. But there's always a trace left behind, a fog remaining. And even if it is erased and we then write over it, even if it's under a thousand layers, there's always something that will betray us, some friction, all in spite of the harmonious gestures and the gentle voice. Because however much you might want to, it is never possible to erase the moment of the crime. There's always that friction, even if only an outline. Even if we later pay visits, bring flowers, write poems. Even if we try to be good. Because there is nothing more dangerous than trying to be good. The certainty that goodness resides in the worst offenses, the greatest injustices in goodness.

But you must know that, right? Who would know that better than you? You, who I forced to be extremely good. From the beginning, from the first look, however good you were, the worse I'd be, or however bad I allowed you to be, the better I would be, like a mathematical equation, the more negatives there are, the more positives, and everything balanced out in the end. Was there a balance between our actions? An equation that was necessary, instantaneous? The more you were, the less I'd be.

Because there was no way of being any different. There was something connecting us, as the extremes of a single piece of apparatus, like the mechanics of a seesaw, it was my weight that raised you up, and just one push from me could bring you back down to earth. Nothing I gave you could be yours without you taking it from me, without my visibly lacking it. And, on the other hand, nothing I ripped out of myself could be anything but yours. Nothing, no joy of mine that didn't mean discouragement, no act of bravery that wasn't a flight. And so I tried hard to be extremely happy, not for the happiness in itself, which I didn't care about, but in order that you might suffer, and to take that something away from you and leave a mark, even if that mark were no more than a cut, a lack. I searched nervously for an unknown happiness, just so that the suffering might at last take shape. I ran through the streets in an unsettled happiness, the wind in my face, I ran and kept running, constant acceleration, and however much you suffered, my will was never calmed, my will never gave in.

I still think of that night every day, that night. Why do we always think about the same things? This will that never gives in. As though the moment continued, happening again and again, as though we were continuing to commit the same crime, all humanity and the whole history of humanity, always the same crime, but there's nothing new about that, is there? I know that's my greatest defeat, that even if I try hard to tell you something new, I'll always just keep saying the same things, even if I make use of the most varied strategies and tell you that they change each time—because time and you and the river passing—even if I make use of the most varied strategies and, like a seductress, tell you there's something that hasn't yet been uttered but which I am telling you now. And I say to you: That night, that last night, remember? Still, I will tell you the same things.

But I'd prefer to start by talking about afterward. Not the precise moment when we were still in the living room, remember? But afterward, when everything had already ended and you went into the bedroom, not a word uttered, you went into the bedroom, lay down on the bed and went to sleep, preventing me from being able to shout, cry, make accusations, point a weapon at you or even leave, or even send you away. For anything I felt or did, you were no longer there, but you were there beside me, as though I didn't exist. But I did exist. Still dressed, or still half naked, as you had left me, those high-heeled sandals, remember? My torso stretched out on the table. Now, in bed, next to you, I hardly moved, my body had become an ovum, a closed structure, my whole body a spiral turning in on itself, silent, still; I avoided any gesture, any doubt, avoided the casual brush of your skin against mine. The brushing of your skin against mine, however lightly, would be a concession, forgiving you silently, after the end, after everything. But to forgive you would be to make your suffering milder, it would be to make your happiness milder. Hatred was what was needed for extreme violence to be consummated, and for love, finally, to be consummated, too.

That's how it often was, what mattered was not the act, however amazing it was, but what came afterward, the two of us lying in bed. And it might be possible to prolong the act endlessly, it might be possible to extend it for a whole stretch of time. The two of us in bed, in my bed, the sheets, your eyes closed. I made my greatest fears eternal and deep, something that kept burning, have I said that already? You never feel the fire at the moment of the flames, just the shock and the memory of other fires, and the expectation of it; only later, once the flames are far off, the flames now extinct, your touch continues to enter deeper. The moment of the crime never exists, didn't I tell you that? Just the sense of some extreme violence. Just a mark on the skin, just a particular tune that comes back again and again. At the time of the pain, it is never possible to feel the pain, or to understand it, or to say, I'm feeling the pain, now, look: the pain. Only later, in bed beside you, the pain opens, deepens, and this happiness of yours that has become complete; only later in bed, next to me, could your happiness be complete. Because no suffering was possible without it meaning some happiness.

The day after our first meeting, I remember I went shopping; you know I like shopping. Not in malls, but walking the streets of the city, crowded with people, the sun or the rain or the wind and the cars going by. I bought a hat. A hat without a brim, tight-fitting, an old-fashioned hat, the kind you only see in photos. I bought it at an antiques shop. A shop hidden at the end of a gallery. Maybe not even an antiques shop, just a heap of old furniture; they sold clothes, jewelry, porcelain dolls, the leftovers of some inheritance or other. The place wasn't well kept, it smelled of mold and cigarettes, and gave the impression that everything there had been left by the side of the street; someone had wandered off and all those objects were just forgotten until somebody else randomly gathered them up.

At the back of the shop, a very thin, very white, very made-up lady was wearing a velvet suit, her black hair tied back, her skin very white, her mouth painted extremely red, her mouth spilling over its edges, as though it wanted to give the lips an unreal outline, a whole face, as though it wanted to give the face another face. This very made-up lady at the back of the store was like a forgotten mannequin. A mannequin who remained back there, ramrod straight, immutable, while outside, the city, and the cars, and the seasons of the year passed by.

As soon as I stepped inside, there was the smell of the long thin cigarette she was smoking in a holder. As soon as she saw me, she made some comment about the hat I was looking at, a black hat, vintage, tight-fitting, like those women used to wear in the twenties; maybe it really was from that period. I asked her, but she didn't answer, she only remarked that my long hair wouldn't go well with that hat, that my long hair didn't go well with my face, she remarked contemptuously, adding that my hairstyle was out of fashion, her thin, delicate hands grabbing a few strands, You'll have to get it cut, she suggested, no, she stated outright, you'll have to cut it, an unavoidable act. I said yes at once, almost not thinking, that I'd cut it really short, just to wear the hat. People nowadays don't have enough style to wear hats, she said, the tone of her voice brusque with clipped enunciation, as though addressing a crowd. I agreed. You have no style either, she went on, looking me up and down disapprovingly; I agreed again. But you could, she said, not attempting to console me. I looked at myself in the mirror, my long hair outside the hat; she was right, this lady, I thought, people have no style.

Try this, she said, showing me a vintage dress, in a velvet like she was wearing, green, an unusual green, an emerald green, a grayish green (is there such a color?). A bit worn at the sleeves, I noticed, but I did as I was told. I took the dress around the back to the fitting room, and she opened the curtain before I'd even finished doing up the front buttons. The top part of the dress looked like a bodice, and some skill was needed to tie the ribbon that zigzagged across the back. She was annoyed at my delay—You're very slow, my dear—and she took the ribbon from my hands, tied the back of the dress closed herself, tightening it till I could barely breathe.

Seeing myself like that, I felt strange. I wanted to laugh, but I looked like an actress in a bit of Poor Theatre, dressed for a role in a long-forgotten period piece. When she saw me, she said, Much better, accompanying the words with a nod of approval, then immediately concluded: The problem is people have no style, she said this several times more. I kept agreeing. Maybe she scared me—I had a feeling that there was no point disagreeing with her. I left the shop with the dress and the hat, paid for with only the vaguest attention to the price; when it was time to pay I said again that, yes, I would get my hair cut, as though apologizing, as though it were a prerequisite for taking the hat. It's for the best, she answered drily, people nowadays, she went on, as I went out the door and walked quickly away along the empty hallway.

I threw the dress away very soon afterward, I don't know why, but even before I'd arrived home. I felt an urgent need to be rid of it, as though suddenly the dress were enclosing a secret, a possibility, so I took it out of the bag and threw it in a trash can in the middle of the sidewalk, spilling out from the top. And at the same time as I feared being discovered, unmasked, I wished with all my strength that someone would see me, someone would see me and save that overflowing green fabric from disappearing.

I kept the hat for some reason; I have it here with me still, in a box at the top of the closet. I never wore it. I never cut my hair. I always thought I would do it one day. Cut it really short, do it myself, and go out wearing the hat at last. Walking along the sidewalk. Whatever the time of day, even in the heat, even under the most burning sun. Feeling as though that one simple change could mean something much more complex. Like now.

That last night lying next to you I thought about that day, strange, isn't it? About that woman, about the dress, about the hat. Perhaps I was trying to tell myself something completely new. Or just to say something without being forced to make use of words filled with meaning. It's impossible to say anything that doesn't have meaning, isn't it? And so even what I'm telling you now, this episode that's so simple, so trivial, I end up involuntarily bestowing some sense on it, a weight.

And so I tell you that on that night, next to you, your closed eyes excluding me, that night it was as though, in some way, I finally had cut my hair really short and gone out onto the street in that hat. And running down the streets, the wind in my face, the hat tightly on, I was looking for my reflection at every opportunity and thinking that this whole time, without realizing it, all I'd done had been planning this moment. And there, next to you, I ran, giving myself up to this moment of no return.

A.

VII

The next morning he was still thinking about the previous day, about how there was no point to keeping watch like that. Not even if he were to spend the whole day there, watching the post office and every woman who went in, every woman who came out, always thinking that each one might be her, and always missing her. How many times had he missed her these past few days, waiting in the snack bar, during some conversation or other, a momentary lapse, a distracted glance. How many times had she been in and out without his even knowing? So close and yet, at the same time, a stranger.

He imagined her tall, very thin, her clothes elegant but

discreet, maybe a little vintage, as though she were right out of an antiques shop, a thrift store, a pearl necklace, he pictured her hair tied back, maybe a few strands come loose, light makeup, the quick walk of someone who knows she is being watched, the walk of someone who has no time to waste. Except for the fact that nobody was her, even if he spent the whole day there, sitting opposite the post office, in the snack bar. Nobody was her, he thought, rather disillusioned.

At last, he decided to talk to the doorman. When he came into the building he asked, as though he didn't really care, it couldn't matter less, he asked whether the doorman knew the previous resident of his apartment; the doorman looked at him suspiciously, first saying yes, then immediately correcting himself to say no, he didn't know who he was, he'd only seen him a few times. He thought it would be best to explain himself, so he explained that some correspondence had arrived addressed to the previous resident and that he didn't know whom to pass it on to; the doorman looked at him strangely—maybe he knew something, he thought—the doorman said he didn't know the new address either, he didn't really know who the former tenant was. And again he felt that the doorman was keeping something from him. Then he thought he was surely being paranoid about this whole business with the letters, what secrets could the doorman and the previous resident really be sharing, after all? He thought it best not to insist. There had to be other ways to get to him, he thought, and he immediately remembered the owner of the apartment, the lady he had only briefly met for the handover of the keys. He would phone her that same day.

He decided to call his ex-wife while it was still early. First, he went into the kitchen and made himself a cup of coffee. He had been eager to try out the machine he'd just bought. He sat on the living room sofa, cup in one hand, telephone in the other. On the end of the line, his ex-wife's irritated voice:

"Hi, Marcos, so you decided to reappear at last."

He drank a gulp of coffee, put the cup down on the coffee table.

"Yeah, I was busy."

"Yeah, I can imagine, you must really be very busy indeed, I've been trying to talk to you for two days, I left you I don't know how many messages."

He looked at the blue envelope on the table, the envelope and the cup, side by side, as though one was not possible without the other, as though in a composition, he thought.

"Yeah, I was busy."

"Sure, but however busy you are, I don't think you should forget you have a daughter, that next week is her birthday and I'm organizing a party."

"Right, I know."

"Look, Marcos, I'm not even asking you to help me organize the party, I'm not asking you to do anything, just that you show up for your daughter's birthday, that's all, it's not as hard as all that, what do you think?"

"Yeah, you're right."

"Excellent, so don't forget, next Wednesday, and as for the present, since you never know what to buy, just leave it to me to buy something, the only thing you've got to do is show up at her preschool. Next Wednesday, four o'clock in the afternoon. You'd better write it down."

He took the envelope carefully, looked closely at it, one more time. The postmark stamped on it.

"Four won't be possible, I'm still at work then."

"Yesterday I called your work at three and you weren't there."

"I was busy."

"Fine, well, next Wednesday you'll also be busy, at your daughter's birthday party."

Resting the phone on his shoulder, with his hands free now he opened the envelope, the letter, five pages, ending, as usual, with just an *A*.

"Fine, you can leave that with me, I'll be there."

"Great."

". . ."

"You know, Marcos, sometimes you're really hard to handle—is there something going on?"

Also as usual, at the beginning of the letter, *My darling*, except that her darling wasn't him, he thought, unable to prevent the feeling of disappointment, perhaps even rage. It wasn't him, but in a way it could be. He put the letter back down on the table.

"No, everything's fine."

"I know you, Marcos, I can sense there's something going on, don't you want to tell me what it is? You never know, I might be able to help."

His ex-wife seemed to have calmed down, at least the tone of her voice was now conciliatory, almost friendly. He tried to reciprocate, to make peace.

"No, thank you, there's nothing going on, really, nothing."

"Are you sure?"

"Yes."

He picked up the cup, took another gulp.

"I mean, yeah, maybe you could help me, actually. Would you mind having Manuela this weekend?"

"What do you mean, have Manu?"

"Just this once."

"Oh, I knew there was something going on, it's that Fabiane, isn't it?"

He looked at the letter on the table, the envelope beside it, he needed a free weekend, he thought.

"No, it's nothing to do with Fabiane, it's just I've got some problems at work, I'm going to have to travel."

"If it isn't Fabiane, who is it, then?"

"I've got some problems at work. That's all it is, nothing to do with Fabiane or any other woman."

"I know you too well for that, Marcos, I know it's some woman, if it isn't Fabiane it's someone else."

It was always the same, he thought, after a few minutes of truce the argument would always begin again.

"I'm telling you there's no woman, would you stop that? I hate how you always insist on thinking you know everything about me."

"Of course I don't, I haven't known anything about you for ages. You became a stranger to me a long time ago."

He got up off the sofa, walked over to the window, it was a sunny day, already pretty hot for that time of the morning. He thought it was the first time since he'd moved to the apartment that he'd had a proper look out of the window.

"So, can you have Manuela this weekend? I'll take her some other time, to make up for it."

After a brief hesitation:

"Okay, I'll do this for you as a favor, but don't get used to it."

They talked a little more, on his part almost out of a sense of obligation, since for some reason his ex-wife bothered him. His ex-wife who barely knew him, that was what she thought. Ever since Manuela was born, they had become strangers, and he was unable to explain what was going on.

He hung up the phone feeling guilty. He didn't call Fabiane back. He didn't return the movies. He didn't go to the office; he'd called in first thing in the morning, a terrible flu, he said, without much conviction. He hadn't gone into the office. Instead there had been the call to his ex-wife.

He felt the anxiety of the previous days when he was leaving the apartment. He called the elevator, but instead of going down to the garage he got out on the first floor, headed for the lobby. This time he wouldn't take the car, this time he'd go out on foot. He greeted the doorman, who responded with a suspicious look. The letter was in his pants pocket, again; he felt strange and naked without the car to protect him from the street, from the people. And it was only at that moment he realized that with the exception of a quick trip to the grocery store or the drugstore, he rarely left home on foot like this.

He looked around him. There was something familiar about the neighborhood, the familiarity of ordinary people, everything there was so ordinary, so normal, it felt like almost a different place, not the one beyond the car window, which was distant, unattainable, the neighborhood he had barely seen since arriving. Since the move. The suitcases and boxes heaped up, many of which he still had not opened, the shelves empty, the whole apartment still unfinished, as though there were something missing, something that would allow him to inhabit the apartment, that would make it finally his. You need some time to arrive anywhere, he thought.

Sometimes, when he was filling in a form, he automatically gave his previous address, the address of the home he'd lived in for so many years with his ex-wife. Separations were always crazy things, his ex-wife felt so distant on the phone, as did his daughter, who would be turning four next Wednesday and for whom he didn't need to buy a present because he had never known how to buy a present for a one-, two- or three-year-old girl, for any birthday. The girl looked at him with the expression of someone complaining, just like his ex-wife, he thought, like Fabiane, he thought, imagining that all women were like this, demanding attention, security, and the expectation of some mysterious thing; he had this feeling of having failed and failing each new woman again.

How about feeling something new, without demands, a

woman ready to give a bit of herself, too, ready to understand that it isn't always possible to be somebody you are
not. A woman ready to surrender something of herself, even
if that something undoes her, transforms her.

He walked on, no longer thinking about any destination
in particular, just wandering around the neighborhood. So
different from the neighborhood where he used to live with
his ex-wife and daughter in a large, airy apartment, with the
countless requirements of a good life.

In this neighborhood, there were old people sitting at
the table of a bar, a restaurant, and the roasted chicken
from the bakery, those simple things, familiar ones, that
had existed in his life and then were lost, he thought as he
wandered aimlessly. He walked on until, on an impulse, he
went into one of the many shopping galleries whose en-
trances it was barely possible to make out, a dark gallery of
stores selling knickknacks and children's clothes, a hair
salon, down at the end an antiques shop, a thrift store, he
thought, not quite sure what a thrift store was. A secondhand clothes store, a green dress, maybe a hat. Isn't that
what he was looking for? He continued down the street,
going into each gallery, the same stores each time, the same
barbers waiting in the doorway, manicurists, people dressed
in black or white. He considered asking someone, Where is

there a secondhand clothes store, a green dress, but he said nothing, he kept walking. Until something caught his eye.

He walked in very cautiously, as though entering a church, a museum, or some other place he didn't know, and in which he didn't know how to behave. He asked himself the same question he'd been asking himself all those days: Why this obsession? And anyway, what was he looking for?

He was asked this by the salesgirl of the shop he had just walked into, a very fair girl with short hair and a slender, delicate face. He smiled coolly, as if she had always known him and was judging him. She stood there, looking at him as though she knew, he thought. But what could she possibly know? He felt uneasy, unable to bear that look, that demand. She reminded him of other girls, not his ex-wife, not Fabiane, but rather girls from an even more distant past. He left without saying a thing, almost ashamed at having gone in. What was he looking for, anyway?—that was the question he was asking himself, too. Something special? An old hat, some dress, a person running into the middle of the street, there was something special he was looking for, yes, something so close, there, maybe in his own life. He went on walking; it had been ages since he'd taken such a long walk, maybe three, four years; it was ages since the city hadn't been merely a landscape seen through the window of the car.

He was trying to summon up the courage, he thought, he was gradually summoning up the courage. But the courage to do what? To face what was to come? To await the next letter? Yes, because he felt there was something in those letters that was approaching. And he was scared, scared to discover it was him, something that he was hiding. You need courage, he thought, to go out like this again, unprotected, unprepared, in the middle of the street. Something was approaching.

It was hot, sweat trickled down his temples, the heat had always bothered him, without the protection of air-conditioning, the heat was becoming a part of him, part of his own body. He was walking fast, nervously, with anxiety. With a trembling that had been forming over the past days and which was increasing in intensity. Or something that had been there for a long time, many years, for a long time already. You need a lot of courage, he thought, a lot of courage, because what would it be like, what would it be like if there was nobody to hold out a hand to him?

His thoughts seemed strange to him, it had already been a few days that his thoughts had seemed strange to him, as though they weren't his, and, at the same time, they had been his forever, he thought. He was walking fast. And he could feel, at last, that something was approaching.

My darling,

Each time I seal the envelope, passing my tongue along the edge of the envelope, it feels so ancient. Have I already told you I get nostalgic for an envelope that is sealed with saliva, something so intimate, a secretion, a final signature? Now I think it might be the only reason for these letters, not the words, not what I say to you, what I make up, what I hide and everything else I might have said to you, not the words, but only the saliva and my tongue sliding over the envelope and the taste that remains for a long time afterward. Just that, I now think. So I say: This is the penultimate letter I shall write you. A farewell? Perhaps. Something completely new, anyway.

The last day. We came back from the rental place and you were silent, then later I was wandering around the house in my pearl necklace. Then I was sitting in front of you, in a chair in front of you, my eyes red, my makeup smudged, the straps of my tank top falling off my shoulders, my hair loose, the way you liked it, remember? I wore those sandals with the really high heels, the pearl necklace, my legs on display; I was thinking about something that would make you smile and suffer, but you weren't suffering. You were there the whole time, sitting on the sofa with a glass of vodka, or maybe it was a glass of whiskey, or of water, I don't know, transformed into something distant, unknown. I didn't know what to say, how to act. And I thought: say something, go sit beside you and take your hand, a casual caress and all would be well, everything would be working again. I sought you out, but your eyes reproached me, and however close I came, there was no way to reach you. And what there was, was this: you sitting on the sofa, the silence spreading and a look in your eyes. I could hear my breathing, the noise of my breathing and the effort in that improvised cadence.

That was how we stayed, you in silence and me breathing—for long minutes the only noise was me breathing. Until my moment of courage: not a full step toward you, but just an attempt, just an infinitesimal movement, an imperceptible suggestion of my approach. At a moment of courage, an imperceptible suggestion, and your immediate response. For the first time that afternoon, you looked me in the eye, a dry look, of hatred? Of rage? How was that possible? You looked at me and said, your voice harsh, your voice changed: Stand up and take off your clothes. An order, remember? Sitting on the sofa, you ordered: Stand up and take off your clothes. Just that: Stand up and take off your clothes. I didn't move, looking at you, my eyes darting away every moment, as though looking at you were a transgression, an arrogance. I was afraid, for the first time, I really was afraid, not like in the morning, not like on the street, your fingers digging into my arm, but a different kind of fear, something much sharper, much more intense.

I stayed there, unmoving, thinking, Why did I go on, why didn't I do anything, why didn't I send you away, or laugh, or shout, or run off. It was as though there were something holding me, as if some voice, some power were holding me and keeping me on that chair, caught, unmoving. For how long? Minutes, hours? Until those same words once again, the same order, and perhaps a forewarning, a threat: Stand up and take off your clothes. How much time had passed, I wonder, before that repetition. Your voice sounded so strange. Tears were running down my face, again, my crying didn't move you, again, but now it was different, now everything was different, even my tears were not so much actual crying, just a prolonged agitation. I felt you looking at me from far away, and with each movement, each detail, the words kept on echoing: Stand up and take off your clothes. My eyes darted away. Your voice hoarse and low, your voice changed. And the whole strength of your absence, of your distance.

I stood up slowly, pushed the chair to one side, so that I remained where I was, and began to take off my clothes. Not with the languor with which you undress for a lover, but as though it were cold and your body was drawing back. My clothes added up to no more than the underwear, the tank top, the sandals with the very high heels and the pearl necklace. I took the top off first, black, tight, the straps falling off my shoulders, did I tell you that already? I moved extremely slowly, and my fingers got all tangled up.

Sometimes I looked over at you, trying to identify what you wanted. But you stayed there, sitting there, unmoving. Looking at me not as a lover sitting across from a woman undressing, but as though someone very heavily clothed were exposing a naked body on a cold day, a naked body to the icy wind, a naked body in the snow.

I took off the top and stood there, unmoving, for a few moments, feeling my breasts as they moved with my breathing, my breasts revealed themselves sensitive and unsettled, decorated with the pearl necklace. I thought that my breasts had never been as naked as they were at that moment, there, in front of you. But there was nothing in your look at all. I was shivering. I stood there, in front of you, the sandals, the underwear, the pearl necklace. My whole body alert. Now you didn't take your eyes off me. Were you angry? I thought, What if it was all just rage? All that was left. Your silence during the day, since we got back from the rental place, since the movie we didn't watch and that character or actor who was so like you, the whole day. And now, this rage, this hatred?

I was standing there, almost naked. You sat on the sofa with your glass of vodka or whiskey, distant, and your voice ordered again: Take everything off, you said, take everything off. You said. But not with expectation or desire, as one might say those words to a half-naked woman, the expectation of the final piece of clothing removed. No. Rather more cutting, more distant. Take everything off, you said. And so I removed the pearl necklace, and as I took off the pearl necklace, it was as though I were losing an important, essential piece, an amulet that would protect and save me, from you, from me, from us. I put it carefully down on the floor, next to me. I was giving up an amulet, a sign, an omen. You sat there saying nothing. I would never say anything again.

Then I took off my underwear slowly, my fingers getting confused. I took off my underwear and left the sandals, the ones with the really high heels, the ones whose straps were tight on my feet, pain spreading up my legs. Now that I come to think about it, I didn't take off the sandals, I didn't take them off and you didn't ask me to. I could have taken them off, I should have, and avoided the extreme nakedness that was a naked body balancing on something unsteady, that uncomfortable position, the straps tight on my feet. A sense of fragility reared up and showed itself. At last, it showed itself.

And when you said, Take everything off, you weren't referring to the sandals, I knew that, and strangely, I obeyed that unspoken order. I could have taken them off, but I didn't, and the underwear ended up as the final piece to go, the one that was left, the underwear thrown down beside me, next to the pearl necklace and the top, a composition on the living room floor, a lure among the floorboards.

I closed my eyes and felt my naked body, my breathing, the rhythm of my breathing giving my body away, and I felt your existence, aggravated. I think now: Being naked wasn't merely not wearing any clothes, being naked was much more arduous, being naked was above all a confrontation, a battle. The nakedness of someone who disposes of an amulet, the nakedness bestowed on me by the high heels, the nakedness bestowed on me by your look, and also the nakedness that brushed against your clothed body, sitting there on the sofa. And I thought that nakedness faced with a clothed body is an unreasonable kind of encounter, an extreme gesture.

Turn to face the other way, you said. The arrogance in your voice. When I turned to face the other way, that was the most intense part, the summit. The height of doubt, of surrender, the height of nakedness, but the highest height was yet to come, we know that, don't we? And I obeyed, once again, I obeyed. And as I turned away, the fear that was new became an ancient fear, my back turned, blind. I would never see you again, I thought, my back was turned and you could do anything: a knife in my back, a gunshot in my back, or even just walk away. I was afraid of your staying; I was afraid of your leaving.

I could turn around at any moment, that constant possibility of freedom, but you knew, didn't you? You sat there, on the sofa, in the distance. And I felt from that distance, your eyes running over my body, your rough, insistent caress. Hours, minutes, on my naked back. My hips. The outlines of my legs. The inside of my legs. Could I be beautiful enough to be like that, naked like that? Could I be strong enough? Could I be coarse enough? Or was it merely fear that kept me like that, as though captive, as though quarry?

Walk over to the table, you said. Remember? The table was right in front of me, the dining table with a jug of flowers on it, a jug of blue flowers. And it was as if I'd forgotten how to walk, moving slowly, one step after another, like somebody taking their first steps, the uncertain steps of a doll, the simple mechanism of a doll. Everything about me was new. And so, naked, I approached the table and the flowers and their jug with the uncertain steps of a doll, until I had come very close, as close as I could, feeling the wood on the skin of my belly, or my thigh. I stood there looking at the blue flowers, blue flowers, I didn't remember having bought them, at the same time there was something so familiar about them, I thought, as my belly felt the caress of the table, and you: a knife, a dagger, some sharp thing in my back.

And then the moment came. Your voice in the distance, your voice changed, your voice commanded me to bend over, you were now only this, an order. My body on the table. My torso stretched out on the table, arms behind me. As if they were tied up, though they weren't. The wood, the jug of flowers. That bending over the table was something that demanded perfect surrender, I thought, and there, surrendered, untouchable, what would we say afterward? When I turned and we faced each other again. I could refuse, my naked body, blind, fragile, tottering on my high heels, I could refuse, but no, I obeyed, and bent over, and felt my breasts adjusting themselves to the wood and to the temperature of the wood, and rested the right side of my face on it carefully, as though I were listening to the sounds of an internal organ, an organ I did not know.

At that moment I still had some hope that you would stop, that you would laugh and say it was all a lie, all a joke, had been all along, ever since the rental place and the movie and the actor, all of it, since breakfast, since everything, a joke, a whim. I still hoped you'd call to me, stroke my face, your words soft and disarmed, a truce, an embrace. And I would be happy, relieved, my head on your chest; I'd tell you that it's okay, it doesn't matter.

But no, your silence continued, my nakedness exposed on the table. Because we always wait right up until the last minute. The imperceptible movement that was you getting up from the sofa, and I felt your body and the heat of your body approaching, and I was a radar, an antenna catching every movement, every outline. And you kept approaching, closer and closer, and I could feel the muffled sound of your bare feet on the wooden floor. Your bare feet. And you said nothing, and I had lost the nerve to ask, I'd never ask again, I thought, my hand never again seeking out yours, any absence, your name, and somebody waving from the other side. My hand seeking out yours.

But I remained where I was, I could have run, but I didn't run, and that was your greatest triumph. Me, lying there, naked on the table, looking at the jug of blue flowers; I was able to run at any moment but I didn't run, not ever.

Behind me, your presence, your breathing. At first, only your fingers were around my neck, heavy and at the same time gentle, as though the whole thing was no more than a lapse, a random act, almost a caress. Then straight after this, do you remember? I wonder if you also sometimes recall this, on a walk, in a meeting or for no reason, just with the passing of time, this memory comes back, because it does keep coming back. Straight afterward, do you remember? Your impossibility. Which had never happened before, that impossibility of yours, you who had exposed me, secret, closed off. Something prevented you, just as desire, just as rage, just as hatred, or the impulse for desire or hatred prevented you, however much you insisted, however much you wanted it, your body refused. At each attempt, your body refused. Or maybe the refusal was mine, that smile, could I have been smiling? Could I be smiling, you thought, mocking this setback of yours, this defeat of yours, with a shy happiness. Our small battle. Me smiling and you standing there, behind me, behind my bent-over body, my secret body, like an altar, like a prayer, silently repeating your name again and again, at every moment. But isn't that just what battles are like? Lost battles. Your greatest defeat. You stood there, unable to take possession of what was yours, offered up to you like that, open, servile.

And then, do you remember? I wonder if you, too, sometimes recall this on a walk, in a meeting, or perhaps for no reason, just with the passing of time, this memory comes back, always comes back. Do you remember what came next? Afterward, when there is nothing left to say? Do you remember? I do. Your desire and its strategies were finally taking shape. Remember? A knife, a dagger, your flesh tearing mine, at last, do you remember? I do. Your flesh tearing mine. Like a weapon. And the tearing of my skin, the most intimate and exposed of my skin. Do you remember? I do.

And I thought, How was that possible, that violence and that fascination, that invasion and that distance. How was it possible? And I gripped hold of the vase of blue flowers as though it, too, were gripping on to someone, but there was only us.

You were holding on to me hard, angry, and from up there, you were looking down at me, thinking me fragile, too fragile, too gentle, too thin, my narrow shoulders, my narrow hips, and the feeling of my being so intimate to you and also now unknown, something lost to you, how was that possible, you thought. Something that should be only yours, you thought, only yours, even if only quick and fleeting in your hands, my neck, which you could squeeze if you wanted to, and the other hand, which you could open, if you wanted to, and my silence, which you could prolong if you wanted to, and the tears you could provoke, and you did want to. An ancient desire, kept secret, hidden away, an act of revenge, something to make me smile or suffer. Because finally you had lost your fear, for the first time, things no longer half finished, something to make me smile or suffer, even if there was something in me that dissipated and died away. Someplace within me, someplace there was you, now, within me; something that was yours, only yours, something that belonged to you; your hands, the delicate border separating us, because that is what love should be, you thought, that's the only thing love could be, an ecstasy, a rapture and one body inside another body, undoing it in an impossible symmetry, you thought, that's the only thing love could be, this conquest, this capture, since now all that was mine was yours, my waiting, my fear and all the joy and all the amazement, and even the words I didn't say were yours, and you thought that this is what love should be when you lose your fear, and there is nothing else that can hurt you, nothing else that can escape you, now that you're capable of anything, now that my disorder is wrapped around you, wound around you. Because ultimately our strength and our weakness and the obsessions and the distance is a line that connects us, as though you had created a shortcut, a bridge, between us, and said again and again, endlessly, that what you wanted was yours now, because that's what love is; when at last we lose our fear, the fear that paralyzes us, the fear that holds us back, we become capable of the most beautiful, the most amazing things, like loving and building a bridge across to another body, and you thought that this should be love after the war and the defeat and the fear, love, that bond that unites us and destroys us, and you thought, that's what love should be, stretching a bridge out and crossing it and destroying it behind you, so that on the other side, in the other body, there's the discovery of something that nothing but pain can appease.

But pain, you thought, pain would never be enough to appease the pain; you gripped hold of me, angry, furious, feeling me getting away, feeling the distance between us, and you held me tight and shouted, your hands surrounding me, that pain, that pain would never be enough to appease the pain, and the desire for something that would make me smile or suffer, something in me, in you, now we are even, this impossible symmetry, my desire yours, my space yours, my defeat yours, our truce, our battles, and you thought that this is what love should be, and realized, frightened, clinging to me, to something within me, that this is what love should be, while on the other side, way over there, out there, I could feel, I could feel, your hand opening, like a rose, like a bud, your hand opening, and hear you exhausted saying that love, that love could never be enough to appease love. To appease love, I heard you say, to appease love, way over there, out there, to appease love, I went on, and when you finished, wanting, thinking, when the desire and the confrontation and the enchantment finally dissipated, when everything finally dissipated and died away, and you moved away, shaking. Frightened? Repentant?

When it was finally all over, and you were covered in secretions and aromas from the inside of another body, my body was bent over the table, open, defeated. You moved away secretly, silently, and left that body there, the enveloping body, the receptacle body. An empty body, there, on the table, gripping on to a vase of blue flowers that wasn't itself gripping on to anything at all.

A.

VIII

The penultimate letter. He sat down on the edge of the bed, the penultimate letter in his hands; he'd been awake all night, it had been years since he'd suffered from insomnia. He usually slept deeply, nothing could disturb him, and something was troubling him now. In the past not even the ringing phone, or a storm, or even an earthquake would wake him, or even Manuela's crying, Manuela the newborn in the next room, Manuela crying the way new-borns cry, that piercing noise, insistent, insistent—he would never wake up, he slept so deeply. Manuela cried all night and you didn't even give me a hand, his ex-wife complained, the milk stains on her white nightie, the milk that never stopped flowing, that mother smell, child smell, newborn-baby smell. But he'd heard nothing, he could have said, I never heard anything, or offered some kind of explanation, but he preferred to keep quiet, he would get up and make a coffee, his ex-wife haggard, bags under her eyes like someone who hasn't slept for days, who has been breastfeeding a newborn baby.

Somebody being born was the most mysterious thing he had ever witnessed, even at a distance. On his way to the hospital he knew that he was useless, empty, there was a feeling that something extraordinary was about to happen, something beyond his control, his ex-wife was having pains, contractions, his ex-wife who would have wanted to squeeze hard on his arm, feel his hand supporting her forehead, hear his voice with soothing words, but he wasn't there, he was walking toward the hospital without ever managing to arrive; his legs became dislocated with every step, like in a nightmare, his mind lost its course, his thoughts disordered, chaotic. Then there was the need for the whole thing to seem normal, the birth, the newborn child wrapped in his arms, and most especially his ex-wife, a body stretched out to the maximum, proud, then later a body deflated, empty; he felt a revulsion he could not confess, but maybe it was just fear, fear of that unknown body his ex-wife had become. How to get close to it again, to its mysteries.

He remembered the only time, after the birth, months

after the birth, the only time, and he thought it strange to be remembering this now, sitting there on the side of the bed, unable to sleep. Baby Manuela was already a bit bigger, sleeping in the next room, crying a bit less, later she practically stopped crying altogether. He remembered the feeling of irritation, the distress, his ex-wife seemed so distant to him, almost a statue, a mask; he remembered that he couldn't do it, his desire unresponsive, refusing, refusing the naked body of his ex-wife, its new roundnesses, its curves, that unexpected sweetness, he couldn't bear its touch, its softness, its depth; his ex-wife lying on the bed, eyes closed, a smile, surrendering, open, that open body, he thought, he felt that same old revulsion: her breasts swollen with milk, the smell that infused the bedroom, and he tried to remember her former body, the one before, slim, supple, the former smell, the small breasts he held in his hands, a breast that disappeared within his hand, the nipple soft, delicate, not like now, he tried with all his might to remake her former body in his mind, that image, his eyes closed, but the touch was different now, the breasts were different, the nipples were dark, coarse, the smell of milk and childhood everywhere, the skin had been stretched out to the maximum, the whole texture of the skin was different now, however hard he tried, it was different. His ex-wife embraced him, wrapped herself around him amorously, perhaps gratefully, with a veiled demand; how could such desire exist in her, such will, a contentment that made her overwhelming and frightening, and nothing he did could change that, and nothing she did could change that, or save him from what she had become.

Sitting there now, on the edge of the bed, the letter in his hands, unable to sleep, he remembered after all these years, he remembered that he had run off, in the middle of the night, got up and got dressed and left, leaving his wife and her desire and her demands. He got dressed and left, he didn't even wait for the elevator or for someone holding the door, he ran down the stairs, far away from himself, far away from everything, and he didn't even think of getting the car; he ran straight past the garage and into the middle of the road, a deserted street, and he ran, trying to think of something, trying to think why he was doing that, why he had left that room and something that should have been his, unique, fragile, because of some fear, as though in that fragility there was unexpected strength, as though his ex-wife might get up and grab a knife and attack him and destroy him, as though she might lose control and could do anything: a dagger, a knife in his back, a fit of anger, an opportunity. A knife, he thought, at any moment, a knife, the blade going into his back, an unknown organ. A thought that, however much he tried to forget it, never left him.

He ran as quickly as he could down the street, imagining that his ex-wife might be behind him, chasing after him, his ex-wife and her moment of madness and the knife and his obsessive thoughts, something possibly stabbed in his back, out on the street, the deserted street; he ran until he couldn't run anymore, his body exhausting itself, gradually slowing, his body growing more and more tired, until he was just there, in the middle of the street, in the middle of the night.

And at that moment, he thought, as he sat there on the edge of the bed, the letter in his hands, at that moment in the middle of the street, in the middle of the night, he thought that something had happened. Sitting here now, on the edge of the bed, the feeling that something had happened, something else, not just his ex-wife with her distended body, the milk flowing from her breasts, no, something more than that, something that was still happening, even now. This obsessive thought kept returning to his mind. He wondered why he was thinking about this now. After all these years.

And bit by bit his body ran dry, until finally it had no strength left, he stopped, looked around him, no longer able to recognize where he was, he looked at himself and no longer knew who he was; he was just a man in the middle of the night, in the middle of the street, for a long time, maybe hours, he never knew, he had no idea where he was, which way to go. Until somebody came up to him, he remembered now, sitting on his bed, unable to sleep—a man, possibly a beggar, he never knew, a man came up to him and asked him some kind of question, was he okay, maybe that was it, was he okay, or could he help, something like that, who was it, a beggar, someone passing by, anyone, and he tried to tell this person that it was nothing, it was fine. He felt bewilderment at not being able to communicate this, at not knowing how, as though he had just unlearned his words, his tongue, language eluding him, he wanted to answer, it's true, he wanted to answer, but there was only that strange dumbness, he wanted to answer but he had unlearned language.

He thought now, sitting on the edge of the bed, at the time, what he had most wanted was to say something, anything, even if it was to ask for help or just to hear the sound of his own voice, even if it was just a primitive, guttural voice, even if it was just the first sound to come out in a tone he didn't yet recognize, beyond his control, even an unexpected voice, but his own voice didn't come out, it disappeared somewhere in his throat. And sitting on his bed, after a night awake, after so many years, he was now thinking about that night; why was he remembering that night, and the man who had been there beside him, a beggar, perhaps, someone who just happened to be passing by, the man had asked him something, something he was never able to answer, because he no longer had words, not even a guttural sound bursting out from his throat, not even that.

The penultimate letter in his hands. The penultimate letter, as though announcing something. And the man was there beside him, possibly a beggar, asking him something, the beggar was getting increasingly insistent, so it seemed to him, asking him the same question again and again in a threatening tone, maybe violent—he wanted to answer, but felt incapable because of something in his throat, his words, his language, and the man came closer and closer, and asked the question again and again, this man wanted something from him, he thought, to take something from him, his thoughts were incoherent, disjointed, he had nothing, and the beggar came ever closer.

He remembered now as he sat on the bed that night, he was in the middle of the street, in the middle of the night, and he remembered vaguely, maybe he had only dreamed it, he thought, vaguely, this memory, just a dream, he thought, sitting there on the bed, awake all night, after such a long time, awake all night and the beggar kept coming closer and the memory was so vague, perhaps it was a beggar, perhaps someone just passing by, he no longer knew, and the certainty that there was something he had to rid himself of, for his own protection, he thought, for his own protection, because everything we do is for our own protection, there never isn't a reason, it's never by chance, just an instinct, a moment of insanity, for our own protection, the beggar was coming closer.

Maybe he didn't have the courage. It was always about courage, he thought, sitting there on the bed, and he was in the middle of the street far away, had there been blood, he asked himself again, how many times had he asked himself, had there been blood, sitting on the edge of the bed, years later, someone shouting, someone crying, someone being born, is that how it was, he wondered, but he didn't know, how could he know—courage, you need courage to allow your memory to appear and install itself—he remembered the road, the lights in the middle of the street, the night, the middle of the night, running, and an obsessive question, the words, the words that disappeared as fast as he could speak them. But now as he sat on the edge of the bed, after the previous night's insomnia, why remember this now, he thought, remembering only halfway, there was always something missing, memory just a nagging question.

Hours later, hours, after arriving home, his wife was in a corner of the room, crying, bags under her eyes, her soft body, her immense body, in a corner of the room, crying, the baby girl sleeping in the next room. His ex-wife cried when she saw him, What happened? she asked again and again, his wife looked at him with that animal look, that animal look, he thought, as though she were seeing him for the first time, as though she saw in him a man disfigured, he thought at that moment and even now, on the edge of the bed, in his room, the letter in his hand, that animal look, the soft body of his wife who asked why, he didn't reply, the words unspeakable, the animal look, he lay down on the bed just as he was, dirty, fully clothed, he didn't even take off his shoes, just as he was, silent, fully clothed, and he slept, that was all, just as he was, he lay down and slept, as though he had just made some very great effort, and his wife was crying, and he fell asleep.

My darling,

What's to be said now, now that I've already said it all?
Now that it's all over. What do we say when everything
is over and the day is dawning and the sheets are stretched
out on the bed, the rumpled sheets, what's to be said in
the next moment, because even after the end there's
something that comes after, something that pulses
and flows? Does something really exist after the end?
Something we don't say, a forgotten word, or a wave, a
gesture left half-finished, something capable of transforming us.

The afterward. Is there an afterward? Separation never
stops. The last time, the endless night, you lying in silence beside me on the bed, or you behind me, sitting
on the sofa, or you, dressed already, headed toward the
door, the last time you headed toward the door in silence,

my hand seeking out yours, something you didn't say but that echoed there, something lost along the way, the people and the cars on the road, your hand on my arm and the mark of your hand on my arm, or long before this, the first look, something lost but that I wanted to be there, secret, still there, something lost infinitely, something unrecoverable but which was still there after everything, after the end. Something capable of transforming us.

Is that it, is that what separation is? I'm alone in this house; is separation a space that appears all of a sudden, the earth unexpectedly opening up, enraged, reconfiguring the landscape, this place where I now find myself? Or is separation just an empty space on the bed? An absence that used to be diffuse and now finally materializes there, beside us on the bed, and faces up to us, merciless, while the night comes into our room. Is that it? And if I were to tell you, no, separation can be anything, not just the earth opening up or an empty space on the bed, but anything, whatever I want, whatever we want, and your space can be any space, even an expectation, a clash, or even a blank space, an envelope, a sheet of paper on which I write these words, where every day I dream up a broad tissue of seductions and questions and answers, patiently, carefully.

There's not just the letters and their epistolary forms, but also another story, that of the reader of these stories. Have I told you about this before? About that other story, this character I've invented, this character with a life so different from yours, someone who receives in error these written words that are directed at you, opens up these pages, careless or curious, and without realizing it, is gradually charmed and transformed. Someone who's so different but who reads me the way I'd like you to read me. And why all of this, you must have been wondering from the start, and again I will answer you: the desire that I should have within me, in my words, something capable of touching you and transforming you, so that you will read me and turn and look at me and, without realizing, create a shortcut, a bridge between us.

So separation can be that, too, you reading on the sofa, or what I imagine you doing, reading on the sofa. My presence. The reflection and reverse of my presence. And I imagine there's something in this game that intrigues you, that surprises you, with every phrase you are surprised and you think, How can I go on here, after everything, you think, How can someone after every-thing, after that night, after the end, the silence, the closing door, how is it possible, this obstinate presence, this tenacity. How could anyone return, go back over the terrain that I go back over in each letter, the interminable separation. And then I tell you that there's always something left over, even after the end, something that insists and returns, in this space I am creating between what I write and what you read, there's a waiting, there's something that transforms us. When we thought every-thing was lost, when we thought everything was over, when nothing else can ever reach us, then it appears, this opportunity to recover the unrecoverable. Because hatred is never only hatred, hatred is never pure, intact, hatred is never only a passion. Something betrays us, something left behind. And what I write to you, these letters, their reflections and reversals, the impulse that started them off is no more than this, what is left behind. The hope that you will turn and look.

Which is why from here, from this space, I imagine that at a certain moment you might come through that door: I'd walk over, my hair loose, wearing high heels, and I see you coming through that door, the interminable separation. At any time of the night, of the day. You ring the doorbell. You walk across the hallway, climbing the stairs. You in the middle of the street. An enchantment. A call.

But why am I telling you this, you might be wondering, and I answer you: Because hatred is never merely a passion, and because you're reading me, because you are still reading me, even now this letter is in your hands, isn't that so? Perhaps, I could answer, because there is something within me that is very beautiful. Something terrible and beautiful. Something of yours, which appears in another space, in another story, so different and which you perhaps do not understand but which belongs to you. Have you thought of that? Something of yours, which belongs to you, even if you don't want it. You carry an emblem, an invisible mark, that only the other person can see and recognize; strange, isn't it? And so this sign I see and recognize and carry, this something of yours in me, makes me keep going. And I tell you that I will be here, every night. Time stretches out and I wait for you, my footsteps in the hall, the doorbell, and you arrive in silence.

So as I hate you, as I try to destroy something of yours in me, there will always be this impulse, this flaw, that I hate you and yet never hate you. The interminable separation. And when you finally return I would receive you—the uneasiness, the doorbell—and I'd take your hand, that same one, the one of the dagger, of the rose that was blooming, the very same, I'd take your hand between my hands, delicately, affectionately, your hand between mine, and I'd close the door and kiss the tips of your fingers, one by one, the tips of your fingers, and then, coming even closer, I'd kiss your forehead, very gently, your forehead, your cheeks, your mouth, at first just our lips brushing together and the breath from your mouth, and I would recognize your taste, as if it were yesterday, the taste of your mouth and your hand between mine. How was that possible? you might be thinking. And I give you my answer: there is something very beautiful in me.

So this is all it's for, this last letter and everything I have written you, just to say that I would receive you, if you returned, if you wanted to, if you, without realizing, were to create a shortcut, a bridge, between us. That's all. I'd receive you without questions, without demands, I'd kiss your hand and lead you to the bedroom, the same bedroom, ours, the same bed, remember? The sheets, the night opening up. The space of the previous night, of the war, the battles lost, I would lead you, withdrawn, silent, and you would go with me and rest your head in my lap, your head weighing on my lap like a stone, my fingers slipping through your hair, the silent tangle of your hair.

And at that moment, everything else will stop mattering, the last day, the last night, the separation, even the letters would lose their purpose, even the possible interpretations, that other story, the words I write you, this glossary of little seductions. All the rest would cease to exist, and nothing would remain but us, us and the forgetting and the calm of forgetting and of defeat. Your head in my lap. I would bend down and kiss your brow, my love, I'd very gently kiss your eyes and the dark color of your eyes, I'd kiss your neck, the back of your neck, I'd feel the taste of your mouth in my mouth and I'd feel in my body the growing velocity of time running on. And I would stay where I was, in that moment, hunched over myself, over us, your head in my lap, your fingers between mine, between my hands, like a knife, between mine, like a knife, my love, and I'm hunched over us, there's something closing, something resting, like a knife, something very beautiful within us, the rumpled sheets, my hair loose, a smile, the dress you like, my skin, my lips, the taste of your mouth.

And you there, so submissive, surrendering, you would ask yourself, how is it possible, all this love. How is it possible?

A.

IX

The insomnia went on. A second night with no sleep. Sleep seemed an unfamiliar comfort to him now, as if it had been years and years, nights following nights, spread out in his memory. The sound of footsteps. A wait.

He got up in the morning, his body tired but alert. He got up in the morning, put on a pair of shorts, a T-shirt, flip-flops, and went downstairs. He didn't even wait for the elevator. The stairs dazed him; he ran down eight flights. He didn't even buy the papers as he usually did on weekends, didn't stop by the market as he usually did; he went straight to the mailbox, and there it was, as he had hoped. He could have spent the night lying in wait, just waiting there all night, waiting for her to arrive, those quick footsteps, that slim body, hair tied back in a bun or a ponytail, he could have spent the whole night there waiting, but no, he was shut away on the eighth floor, wide-eyed with insomnia. All night long he knew that she was approaching once more, that she was walking into the building, crossing the hall over to the mailbox, putting an envelope through the narrow slit, with his address and a different name. The next morning, there it was, the last letter, a presence lingering.

He waited till he was back home, upstairs, before opening the envelope, the envelope that had seemed like it would never come, the blue envelope that enclosed a whole journey, an expectation. A whole night of insomnia. Somebody greeted him in the elevator but he was silent, his head down, he didn't even smile, as though any gesture, any word could break this most fragile of links, this strange communication that had begun. Any word. The closeness of the moment had stretched out during his nighttime vigil, waiting for him. His sweating hands stained the envelope, the ink from the envelope on his fingers, the ink from a different name. He got out of the elevator. He walked into his apartment, closed the door, feeling safe as he closed the door, and at the same time feeling fear that at any moment somebody might burst in. He went into the apartment, put his keys down on the table, the envelope in his hands; he opened it carefully, sat down on the first chair he came to and there he stayed. The open letter stretching, lengthening. The open letter and time passing, beside him, time approached him and touched him, without ever really reaching him.

And as he read, for the first time in those recent few days, there was something that was his. It was as though she had moved, the direction of her voice, of the wind: she addressed him for the first time, really addressed him, it was no longer a mistake, no longer an appropriation. She wrote to him, holding out her hand. She was waiting for him. Not like his ex-wife, not like Fabiane, not like the others who came and went, even Manuela, a three-year-old girl, not like the world that surrounded him and made its demands, but a different movement, a different capacity; she was waiting for him and she held out her hand, he thought, she held out her hand, in spite of everything, in spite of the worst crimes, not in exchange for anything. How was that possible? Because it was him, not anyone else, not a stranger or an actor who looks like him, not just anyone, and if he had seen himself in the mirror at that moment, he would have been able to see himself—he was sure of it—if he looked at himself in the mirror, he would see a new face, the face of someone who has spent the last few nights awake. His face in the morning. He who'd always slept so well. He who had been transformed, something in him had been transformed and had emerged as a different image. His face. How was it possible, he asked himself.

Without her realizing it, everything had scattered and stretched for him. The rounded handwriting on the envelope, the fountain pen, the nostalgia for getting ink between your fingers, a whole past: she might be anybody, any woman, anyone who might walk past him and smile while he's standing outside the post office, waiting in the street. Him, any man, waiting for her. He pictured this woman, very thin, almost ethereal, from the height of those heels, the dress he so liked, the loose hair falling over her face, a dark curtain. That woman who was so fragile, holding out her hand to him. Time passing. Slender fingers, ink, saliva to close the envelope, nostalgia, a secretion. And at the same time, something in the letter scared him. That woman, so fragile. How was that possible, he thought.

And there he stayed, afraid to make any movement, any gesture, afraid of anything that might break this suspended moment, this spell. Slowly, he was feeling as though something was starting to belong to him. And he felt something that was his in that letter, it was no longer just addressed to another person, with another secret, another declaration, but it was something addressed to him, something that was his. And he felt that his eyes were not obeying him, looking in every direction, sensing a whole desire he had no way of

fulfilling, because things were happening without his com-
prehension, he thought.

He thought he needed to do something, at last, to act.
Not just linger at the snack bar any longer, or check out the
movie, or go by the antiques shop, or the post office, no
more waiting and silence, but he had to do something real.
Something real, at last, he thought. And he picked up his
phone.

The owner of the apartment had a house outside the city
and was hardly ever around. She spent her weekends up in
the mountains. With the views and mild climate of the
mountains. He had seen her only once, for the handover of
the keys. She was a woman with very well styled red hair.
Dressed in a suit and accessorized with a number of brace-
lets and rings. An impeccable lady, she reminded him of his
own mother-in-law, and what his ex-wife would probably
become in fifteen, twenty years, another impeccable lady.

He looked at the envelope, which at that moment seemed
such a strange object. The letter on the table. The sheets of
paper, the whole thing so nostalgic; he wasn't even finished
moving in, the apartment was still pretty much empty,
boxed up.

On the phone the impeccable lady seemed surprised to
hear from him on a Sunday, at that time of the morning,
but it couldn't wait till Monday, it was urgent, he explained,

trying to find the words that would sound serious, thought-
ful, elegant. What could be so pressing as to make him call
on a Sunday morning at that time—she seemed annoyed
behind her apparent politeness, and he apologized again,
talked about the letter, there had been a delivery, an urgent
letter, and wasn't that the former tenant's name? It was, yes,
replied the lady on the other end, surprised in her house in
the mountains. So someone who didn't know that he'd
moved had sent him something urgent, something old-
fashioned, a letter, a letter, the owner thought this strange,
a letter on a Sunday morning. That's right, he replied, so
you can see how urgent it is, he felt ridiculous saying this.

It felt childish saying this to her. Manuela would have
once again watched him with disappointment from her
lofty three years. There was a brief pause at the other end,
And what do you want me to do about it, she replied at last.
Nothing, he said, but I got worried that it was something
really important, he said without needing to lie. It is something terribly important, he thought, making him feel almost childish in that ridiculous situation on a Sunday
morning, and he recalled Manuela and her implacable
gaze, that image of the inquisitive little girl. There's nothing I can do, the impeccable lady concluded, but I can, he
said, I could call and let him know; he tried to sound uninterested. Manuela was always so blasé, she'd be terrifying at

fifteen, and why was he thinking about this right now, he thought. Or I could even deliver the letter myself, if he isn't too far away, he added carefully. She was surprised, the impeccable lady: You could do that? Of course, he replied, almost glad, of course I would. It was somebody so different, someone waiting for him, holding out a hand, he thought. But he just said yes, he'd let him know if she would give him the new phone number, but no, she didn't have the number there, it was in her other address book, she'd left it in the city; the impeccable lady was in her house in the mountains. He paused and said nothing; somebody was waiting for him, for the first time, and he felt one wrong word and he would lose all the ground he had just gained. Then she offered, I do have the address, if you really don't mind, and he waited a few seconds, If it isn't too far, he said, terribly afraid that it would be, yes, very far, but she said no, it's very close. He thought, things are so easy sometimes, things were happening, somebody was waiting for him, and he felt unsettled. How was this possible? But he went on, of course, I'll stop by, I'll leave it with the doorman; the owner was pleased, Very good, most kind of you, perfect, she concluded, nowadays people don't worry about one another anymore, they can be so selfish, you know, and he smiled, it had been such a long time, he agreed, It's no trouble at all, since it's so close by, the letter open on the table, the blue envelope, when I go out to pick up my daughter I'll stop by, the little girl so distant, but that didn't matter now, I'll leave it at the front desk. It's no trouble at all, and she said, But people are so selfish, so when I come across somebody like you, of course, I just think, and she went on. And he thought of Manuela again, her inquiring gaze, this conversation that wouldn't end, so early on a Sunday morning, this impeccable lady.

When he finally hung up, he had the bit of paper, at last, with the address and all its possibilities, and he put it in his pocket and went out. Just as he was, shorts, flip-flops, T-shirt, hair uncombed, his face still a mess from a sleepless night. He ran down the stairs. The address was in his pocket and he had a bundle of letters in his hands: nine letters, one for each day. The blue envelopes. The rounded handwriting. He got in the car, and anxiety began to settle in. The address on a bit of paper. That whole time he hadn't really thought about what he was going to do when the time came, when the time finally came. What would he say, the bundle of letters open in his hands, the letters consumed, spent, read.

He drove on without thinking. The Sunday morning streets still empty. He could even forget about the whole business, chalk it up to one of those things that happen so quickly and then we just forget about them, but he didn't want to, he wanted to go up the steps, or in the elevator, the elevator of the building that was nearby, no more than five, ten minutes' drive, the woman had said on the phone, ring the bell and stand there with that bundle of letters, looking at the man on the other side of the door, as though looking in a mirror, looking closely, as though seeing something unexpected. And when this man saw the envelopes, the handwriting, and when he saw the envelopes open and the letters read, what would he say to him, that it had been by accident, that he'd opened nine letters by accident, because that's how things happen, real things.

He'd say the letters were his, that they were his now, and he wouldn't be lying. He would ask for the address, the return address that was never there, and the name, just an initial. He would say, correctly, that they were his now, they belonged to him, and what would the man on the other side say, as if in a mirror, he wondered. He was someone who left, because after all this was the man who had left, who had run away, running down the middle of the street, in the early morning, but not him, he'd stayed, he was there now, the open letters in his hands, in his hands, he would show them to him, what was now his, she was waiting for him, for him, and he would be the one to lie down in her lap, his head heavy as a stone in her lap after the battle, he'd say, looking at the other man like someone seeing himself and, at last, recognizing himself. He would say it was his, all those days, those words, that he'd been looking for her, right across the city, he'd been looking for her, him, the apartment, the movie, a cup of coffee, everything that belonged to him.

And so, when he took a good look at that man on the other side of the door, he would see nobody. He would ring the bell, the door would open, and there would be no one there.

When the man finally opened the door, it wasn't him, that was the first thing he thought, surprised. He was in jeans and a T-shirt, any old man, a guy like so many others. This man gave him a look that was not exactly friendly. He was standing there on his doorstep, after all, early on a Sunday morning.

What letters are those, the man asked with a certain brusqueness. He had already explained on the intercom who he was and what he had come for, about the owner of the apartment, the address, the urgency, and he just stood there a few seconds, as though he himself didn't know the right answer. What are those letters, he asked again. The letters weighed down his hands. He held out one of them, an envelope. Just one. The man took the envelope, examined it with curiosity, yet didn't hide a certain impatience at the open envelope, somebody else's letters. He wore an expression of distrust and reproach. He looked at the address, the sender, opened the letter, the letter a foreign body. He read it then and there, quickly, standing in front of him like a mirror, he thought. The man standing in front of him read the words he knew by heart, the pauses, the rhythms. He watched each gesture, each change of expression, however small, something that might give him away. He watched his hands, his fingers holding the paper, as if they meant something, and they did. He had read and knew every space, every line. And as the man read, it was as though the whole world were suspended; as he read, everything was still possible. He felt his breathing speeding up, his whole body contracting, his whole body waiting.

And when the reading was over, everything went back to regular existence.

"What does this mean?" The man held out the letter, the envelope, as though using the gesture to punctuate his question.

He was still standing there, unsure how to reply. Then he said:

"It's a letter."

"Yeah, that much I get."

"It's . . ."

"What does this mean?" His voice was turning impatient. "Some kind of joke?"

He rushed to make himself clear:

"No, of course not."

The man looked at him suspiciously. He tried to explain:

"Is that not you? It's got your name on it, the address . . ."

"Of course it's me. But these letters aren't for me. These letters, which—by the way—you've already opened, read, done whatever you wanted with, haven't you?"

"Yeah, I'm sorry, I . . ."

"Well, I'm not the person you have to apologize to. These letters aren't mine. In fact, I have no idea who she is, this woman."

He looked at the letter one more time:

"It's not even signed."

"No, that's right."

"And now that I look more carefully, my name doesn't appear in the letters, only on the envelope, or is it in the other letters?"

"No, it isn't."

"Well then?"

He didn't know how to reply.

"You don't want to take a look at the others?"

"No. What for? I'm telling you they aren't for me." His voice brusque, irritated.

Then, more conciliatory:

"Look, it must be some joke, some hoax, whatever."

"A joke?"

"Yeah, someone's playing a joke on you, I guess."

"On me?"

The man nodded. He kept insisting:

"You're absolutely sure the letters aren't yours?"

"Absolutely."

"But this woman, you don't know her?"

"No."

"But don't you have any idea who she might be? You only read the first letter, if you read the others I'm sure that maybe . . ."

What had been impatience was beginning to turn into aggression:

"Look, are you deaf? I'm telling you I don't know her, I don't know who she is, I've never seen her, I'm not interested, I have no idea at all. And I've got better things to do than to stand here reading this pile of letters some crazy woman has decided to write."

He stood there, looking at him as if he were no longer there.

"Look, I'm really sorry, but I've got things to do. You've

come here, I've seen you, I've explained things. Thank you for the trouble, thank you for coming, it's all great, but I've got to go now."

"Ah, of course . . ."

"Here's your letter, look, it must have been some kind of joke."

"Sure, a joke, of course."

The man closed the door, and he stayed there a while, the door closed to him. As though there were still a possibility of the man changing his mind, his memory returning, something he'd forgotten to say, or at least a clue, a curiosity. He felt heavy, the stress was only now starting to reveal itself. His own thoughts, the difficulty in getting them to take shape, kept disappearing before they even became a series of words or an intention. Eventually he gave up. He turned with some effort and made his way slowly toward the elevator. The bundle of letters still in his hands. The bundle of open letters, the blue envelopes, from one moment to the next, had lost their meaning, the meaning he had given them. These past days without sleep. And now there was not even any more waiting to do.

In the meantime, the street was full of busy people and their newspapers and loaves of bread and milk they had just bought.

He was moving slowly. The elevator door opened and he

got in, pressed a button, stepped out, walked past the door-man without looking to either side, past the metal fence at the entrance and out onto the street. There was a hubbub of cars and people. The hubbub of a Sunday that was finally starting. And he kept on walking, as though he couldn't hear it, or as though the sounds reached him muffled, the pack of open letters weighing him down, his steps weighing him down, his steps getting slower and slower. On his face, an involuntary grimace, a vein standing out, his hair cling-ing to his forehead.

He had been carrying the letters, had spent the whole week waiting, endured the recent days' insomnia, and some-thing dissolved away, right there, in his hands. The letters and everything dissolved away into the distance. The land-scape, the cars and the muffled noise of the cars, and the people and the muffled noise of the people, all around him, and everything around him, circling, circling, at that early time of the morning. How was it possible. That urgency. How was it possible. That encounter, that battle.

How was it possible, he thought.